OTHELLO

SILVER EDITION

WILLIAM SHAKESPEARE

EDITED BY
ADAPTIVE READER

ISBN: 979-8-8693-0821-4

CONTENTS

INTRODUCTION

Welcome to Adaptive Reader, your portal to the captivating world of literature, tailored to fit your unique reading abilities.

In today's fast-paced and diverse learning environment, we believe in the power of personalized learning experiences. That's where the concept of leveled reading comes in, and why we, at Adaptive Reader, have dedicated ourselves to offering a broad collection of classic novels at various reading levels. Our mission is to make the joy and benefits of reading accessible to everyone.

THE BENEFITS OF LEVELED TEXTS

So, what exactly is leveled reading? It's an approach that matches students with texts that align with their unique reading abilities. This ensures that every reader is challenged just the right amount - enough to grow, but not so much that they feel overwhelmed or frustrated.

For students, this means you'll engage with texts that stretch your reading skills while keeping the experience enjoyable and manageable. You'll gain confidence as you successfully comprehend each level and feel motivated to explore more challenging texts as your reading skills grow.

For teachers, Adaptive Reader provides a valuable tool to support differentiated instruction. You can assign the same novel to your entire class while ensuring each student reads a version that aligns with their reading level. This allows all students to participate in class discussions and activities, fostering a more inclusive learning environment.

For parents, Adaptive Reader offers a supportive tool to encourage your children's reading journey. As your child progresses through the different levels of a novel, they'll not only enhance their reading skills but also develop a deeper love for literature.

READING ACROSS MULTIPLE EDITIONS

All of our leveled novels include passage markers that correspond to the same content across every one of our editions. This means that passage '62' in our silver edition contains the same themes and plot elements as passage '62' in our original edition.

For teachers, this means that you can say "let's look at passage 35 together. What is the author trying to tell us here?" and all of your students will be reading the same content — but with vocabulary and syntax that's adapted to their reading level.

Our online reading tool, available at www.adaptivereader.com, gives students and teachers free access to the original text with passage markers. We encourage teachers to include close readings of the original text as part of their coursework, giving all students exposure to the rich original syntax and language of these exceptional authors.

THE POWER OF LITERATURE

At Adaptive Reader, we are committed to helping everyone experience the power of literature. So whether you're a student diving into a classic novel, a teacher looking for flexible resources, or a parent seeking ways to support your child's literacy, Adaptive Reader is here for you.

We invite you to embark on this exciting literary journey with us. Enjoy the world of stories, characters, and ideas that await you in our collection of leveled novels. Happy reading!

DRAMATIS PERSONÆ

DUKE OF VENICE: Leader in Venice.

BRABANTIO: Leader in Venice and Desdemona's father.

GRATIANO: Brabantio's brother.

LODOVICO: Brabantio's relative.

OTHELLO: A war hero who works for Venice.

CASSIO: Othello's lieutenant.

IAGO: A man who holds up Othello's flag during battle.

MONTANO: The war hero *before* Othello.

RODERIGO: A gentleman from Venice

CLOWN: Othello's helper.

DESDEMONA: Brabantio's daughter and Othello's wife.

EMILIA: Iago's wife.

BIANCA: Cassio's girlfriend.

Others: Sailors, Messengers, Clowns, and more.

SCENE: The first act takes place in Venice. The rest of the play is in Cyprus at a Seaport.

ACT I

SCENE 1. VENICE. A STREET.

 [Enter Roderigo and Iago.]

RODERIGO:

Don't even start!

I'm pretty upset with you, Iago.

I let you use my money like it was yours.

IAGO:

I didn't do it. I'm telling you.

If I did such a thing, you'd find a reason to hate me anyhow.

RODERIGO:

You told me once that you really dislike him.

IAGO:

If that's not true then you can hate me.

Let me tell you why:

I had three important people in the city

Who personally wanted to help me become his assistant.

They went ahead and recommended me for the job.

I know I'm good enough for it. But you know what he thinks?

He thinks highly of himself and doesn't want to listen to them.
He says he's already picked someone else for the job.
And who is this person? Apparently,
A great mathematician named Michael Cassio, from Florence.
Sure, he has a beautiful wife,
But he has never actually led troops into battle.
He doesn't know much about actual battle strategies
Anymore than a housemaid. It's like he's great at talking like a soldier,
But not at actually being one. But he was chosen for the job.
And me, even though he's seen what I can do in
Places like Rhodes and Cyprus,
I must now stay quiet and take orders from this bookworm.
RODERIGO:
Well, I hope to be his executioner.
IAGO:
Well, there's not much we can do about it.
It's the downside of serving others.
It seems like the only way to get ahead
Is to know someone or the right person.
Now you, sir, decide for yourself
Whether it's right for me to be loyal to the Moor,
The man we speak of.
RODERIGO:
Personally, I wouldn't choose to be a loyal follower.
IAGO:
Oh, take it easy, sir.
I follow him only because it serves my own interests.
Not everyone can be a leader, and not all leaders
Can get respect. You will see
Many hardworking servants
Wasting their lives like donkeys.
But there's not point. They'll eventually be fired
When they can no longer do the job.

But there are some servant who are really smart.

They work hard and pretend to be loyal,

Yet focus on their own interests.

When they've gotten what they wanted, like money,

They show how smart they've been all along.

These fellows have some spirit,

And I declare myself one of them. Because, sir,

As sure as your name is Roderigo,

If I were the Moor, I certainly wouldn't be Iago.

In following him, I'm really just looking out for myself.

Heaven is my judge, not love and duty.

I just need to look loyal on the outside.

But I will wear my heart upon my sleeve.

Birds will peck at it. But the truth is: I am not what I am.

RODERIGO:

What a lucky guy this is. He can get away with this!

IAGO:

Let's move on: wake up her father.

Disturb his peace, ruin his joy and tell everyone about the Moor.

Even if he seems happy, disrupt him.

Bring troubling news to him.

RODERIGO:

Here's her dad's house. I'll shout to him now.

IAGO:

Go ahead, but make sure you sound scared

And worried, like a person alerting others of a fire!

RODERIGO:

Hey, Brabantio! Mr. Brabantio, wake up!

IAGO:

Wake up! Brabantio! Thieves, thieves!

Look after your house, your daughter and your money!

Thieves, thieves!

Brabantio appears above at a window.

BRABANTIO:

What's all this shouting about? What's going on?

RODERIGO:

Sir, is your whole family safe indoors?

IAGO:

Have you locked your doors?

BRABANTIO:

Why do you ask that?

IAGO:

You've been robbed!

Quickly, put on your robe.

Right now, at this very moment,

An old black ram is with your pure white ewe.

Wake up, ring the alarm bell!

Or else you'll be a grandfather before you want to be! Get up, I said!

BRABANTIO:

Have you lost your mind?

RODERIGO:

Respected sir, do you recognize my voice?

BRABANTIO:

Not me. Who are you?

RODERIGO:

My name is Roderigo.

BRABANTIO:

I told you not to hang around my home.

My daughter is not interested in you.

Now you've shown up

Ready to disturb my peace?

RODERIGO:

Sir, sir, sir,...

BRABANTIO:

Be aware,

My position and power can make things difficult for you.

RODERIGO:

Patience, good sir.

BRABANTIO:

What do you mean by "robbery?"

This is Venice.

RODERIGO:

Honorable Brabantio,

I come to you with good intentions.

IAGO:

Sir, you're being unreasonable. We are here to help, but you think of us as thugs. Keep this up and your daughter will end up with a stranger. Your relatives will be strangers to you too.

BRABANTIO:

Who are you, vile person?

IAGO:

I am someone who's here to tell you your daughter and the Moor are now together romantically.

BRABANTIO:

You are a villain.

IAGO:

And you are a senator.

BRABANTIO:

You will answer for this. I recognize you, Roderigo.

RODERIGO:

Sir, I will explain everything. But I beg you to listen.

Your beautiful daughter,

At this late and sleepy hour of the night,

Took a gondola ride to see the Moor.

If you allowed this, we are sorry for intruding.

But if you weren't aware, we've been yelled at

For no reason.

I would not make a joke of respect.

Your daughter (if you didn't give her permission)

I say again, has made a big mistake.

She's bet her duty, beauty, wit, and riches

On a wild and random stranger.
Immediately find out for yourself
If she's in her room or your house.
If she is, I can be punished for misleading you.

BRABANTIO:
Give me a lantern! Round up all my people!
This situation is just like my dream,
Believing this weighs me down already.

Exit from above.

IAGO:
Goodbye. I must leave you now.
It doesn't seem right or healthy for my position
To be found. If I stay, it will cause a fight with the Moor.
I know what will happen anyway.
Even though this may upset Brabantio,
He cannot fire the Moor because he
Will lead us in the Cyprus wars.
We have no one else.
Even though I hate him,
I must make it seem like I like him.
Which is really just a symbol. You will surely find him,
Guide the search party,
And I will meet him there. So, goodbye.

Exit. Enter Brabantio, with Servants and torches.

BRABANTIO:
This is too much of a terrible truth. My daughter is gone,
And what's ahead in my unfortunate days,
Is nothing but unhappiness. Now Roderigo,
Where did you see her? (Oh, my poor little girl!)
With the Moor, did you say? (Who'd want to be a father!)
How did you know it was her? (Oh, she fooled me
Beyond my wildest thoughts.) What did she say to you? Get more torches,
Gather all my family. Do you think they are married?

RODERIGO:

Honestly, I believe they are.

BRABANTIO:

Oh no! How did she escape? Oh, my heart is betrayed!

Fathers, from now on do not trust your daughters' actions

By what you see them doing. Aren't there tricks

By which the innocence of youth and girlhood

Can be taken advantage of? Haven't you heard, Roderigo,

Of something like this happening?

RODERIGO:

Yes, sir, I have indeed.

BRABANTIO:

Call my brother. Oh, I wish you could've had her instead!

Some how, some way. Do you know

Where we can find her and the Moor?

RODERIGO:

I believe I can locate him, if you're willing

To get some guards, and accompany me.

BRABANTIO:

Please lead the way. At every house I'll knock,

I have the most authority here. Get weapons, everyone!

Prepare some special nighttime guards.

Let's go, good Roderigo. I will reward your efforts.

Exit.

SCENE 11. VENICE. ANOTHER STREET

[Othello, Iago, and their friends enter with torches.]

IAGO:

Although in battles I've killed men,

I could never plot a murder.

I don't think I have that evil inside me.

Although, I really wanted to hurt him.

OTHELLO:

It's better this way.

IAGO:

No! If you had heard what he was saying about you,

You would understand how hard it is to ignore.

Anyhow, I must ask you, sir,

Are you securely married? Because you should know this,

That this man is loved his words impact others.

He can separate or use the law against you.

OTHELLO:

Let him try his worst.

My services, which I have done for the government,

Will silence his complaints.

My life and existence

Are given to me from men of royal rank. And my worthiness

Can match a fortune

Like the one I've achieved. Know this...

I love Desdemona so much I'm willing to give up my freedom.

But look, who's coming there with lights?

IAGO:

It's her upset father and his friends.

You'd better go inside.

OTHELLO:

I'm not hiding. I'm honest and have

Nothing to be afraid of. Can you see them?

IAGO:

I don't think so.

Enter Cassio and Officers with torches.

OTHELLO:

The duke's servants and my deputy.

A wonderful night to you, friends!

What's the news?

CASSIO:

The duke sends you his greeting

And he needs you to go to him right away.

OTHELLO:

What do you think the problem is?

CASSIO:

Something from Cyprus, as I can tell.

It seems urgent. The ships

Have sent a dozen messages.

One right after the other tonight

And many of the council members

Are already with the duke. You've been urgently called for.

When you weren't at your house,

The senate sent three different search parties
To find you.
OTHELLO:
It's good you found me.
I will just say a word here in the house,
And then I'll go with you.

Exit.

CASSIO:
Iago, why is he here?
IAGO:
Well, tonight he has won a big prize on land.
If it's legal, he's set for life.
CASSIO:
I don't understand.
IAGO:
He's gotten married.
CASSIO:
To who?

Enter Othello.

IAGO:
Come, captain, shall we go?
OTHELLO:
Let's go.
CASSIO:
Here comes another group looking for you.

Enter Brabantio, Roderigo and Officers
with torches and weapons.

IAGO:
It is Brabantio. General, watch out.
He's here with bad intentions.
OTHELLO:
Hey, stop there!
RODERIGO:
Sir, there's Othello.

10

BRABANTIO:
Take him down, thief!

They start to fight.

IAGO:
You, Roderigo! I can handle you.

OTHELLO:
Put your swords away.
Kind sir, you'll get more respect with kindness
Than with your weapons.

BRABANTIO:
Where is my daughter, you wicked thief?
You must have cast a spell on her,
Because I can't believe for a second
That such a young, beautiful, and sensible girl,
Who hasn't even wanted to get married would leave
Everything she knows and run off to marry you... a thing like you.
This is a marriage out of fear, not joy.
Let the world judge me if it's not an easy thing to believe.
I think you have used evil magic on her.
I will get to the bottom of this.
That's why I arrest you:
For being a threat to everyone and practicing forbidden magic.
You take him, and if he fights, stop him.

OTHELLO:
Stop. All of you, whether you're on my side or not!
If I was supposed to fight, I'd know it.
Where do you want me to go to answer these charges?

BRABANTIO:
You can go to jail until we can go to court.

OTHELLO:
What if I agree to answer your questions?
And I ask: How will the duke like that
I'm doing this instead of going to meet him?
He's just sent messengers to get me.

OFFICER:
That's true, sir,
The duke's in a meeting, and I'm sure,
You're being called for.
BRABANTIO:
What? The duke in a meeting?
This late at night? Take him away.
My issue is serious. The duke himself,
Or any of my fellow lawmakers,
Must surely feel this pain like it is their own.
Our leaders will not be able to let this go.

Exit.

SCENE III. VENICE. A COUNCIL CHAMBER

[Enter the Duke and Senators sit at a table, with Officers close by.]

DUKE:

The news we've received just doesn't seem right.

FIRST SENATOR:

You're right, they don't match. My letters mention a hundred and seven ships.

DUKE:

Mine mention a hundred and forty.

SECOND SENATOR:

Mine say two hundred.

Even if the reports don't exactly match,

They all confirm a Turkish fleet of ships is coming to Cyprus.

DUKE:

It's possible, I suppose.

I don't want to rush to conclusions,

but I agree this is scary.

SAILOR:

[From off stage.] Hello! Anyone there?
OFFICER:
A message from the ships.

Enter Sailor.

DUKE:
Alright, what's the information?
SAILOR:
The Turks are preparing to attack Rhodes.
The message comes from Signior Angelo.
DUKE:
What do you think about this?
FIRST SENATOR:
This can't be true.
It does not make sense. It's a trick.
We should think about the importance of Cyprus to the Turks.
If Cyprus is less protected than Rhodes,
It's easier for Turks to attack there.
We should not underestimate the Turks.
He might be ignoring an easier, more rewarding route,
To challenge a danger that won't benefit him at all.
DUKE:
I don't think he'll go for Rhodes.
OFFICER:
I have more news.

Enter the Messenger.

MESSENGER:
The Ottomites, respectful and powerful,
Sailing toward the island of Rhodes,
Have met up with another fleet there.
FIRST SENATOR:
Ah, just as I thought. How many ships, would you guess?
MESSENGER:
There are around thirty ships, and they've now changed
Their course, openly showing

Their intention to head for Cyprus. Signior Montano,

Your faithful and brave servant,

Sends his regards through me,

And asks you to trust him.

DUKE:

It's settled then, they're heading for Cyprus.

Is Marcus Luccicos in town?

FIRST SENATOR:

He's currently in Florence.

DUKE:

Write to him from us and send the message quickly.

FIRST SENATOR:

Here comes Brabantio and the brave Moor.

Enter Brabantio, Othello, Iago, Roderigo, and Officers.

DUKE:

Brave Othello, we need your help

Against the common enemy, the Ottomans.

[To Brabantio.] I didn't see you. Welcome, kind sir,

We missed your advice and your help tonight.

BRABANTIO:

And I missed yours. Please forgive me, your grace.

I was not aware of anything that required my attention.

Plus, my personal sadness is distracting me.

And it's still the same as it always was.

DUKE:

Wait, what's the problem?

BRABANTIO:

My daughter! Oh, my poor daughter!

DUKE and **SENATORS:**

She's dead?

BRABANTIO:

To me, yes.

She has been stolen from me. She's been manipulated

by tricks, potions, and a fraud.

DUKE:

Whoever he may be,

Know that he will face justice.

You will see the strict rules of the law in action,

Even if our very own son

Were involved in this action.

BRABANTIO:

I sincerely thank you, Duke.

Here stands the man, this Moor.

He is now here to hear about state affairs.

ALL:

We are saddened by the situation.

DUKE:

[*To Othello.*] How do you respond?

BRABANTIO:

I can't say anything but the truth.

OTHELLO:

Honorable and respected gentlemen,

I admit that I have indeed married this man's daughter.

The scope of my wrongful action stops there.

I don't have a fancy vocabulary, since

I'm not used to talking about peaceful matters.

For seven years until now,

My efforts have been dedicated to warfare,

And I know little about the larger world,

Other than about fights and battles.

15 **OTHELLO**:

I might not improve things by speaking about myself.

Still, if you will listen,

I will honestly describe

My entire love journey and how

I won his daughter's hand.

BRABANTIO:

She was never like this.

She was so calm and quiet that she would blush at her own actions.

And she, despite everything,

Fell in love with something she used to fear to look at?

It's like she was tricked!

This is a plan from hell.

That's why this situation occurred. I want to repeat

That the love potions were used to trick her.

DUKE:

Saying this isn't proof.

We need more evidence of this.

FIRST SENATOR:

Othello, tell us:

Did you dishonestly and forcefully

Capture and corrupt this young girl's feelings?

Or did it naturally come from her, with such honest intentions

As two souls could share?

OTHELLO:

I respectably request that you

Bring the lady here.

Let her speak about me in front of her father.

If you find any misdeed in her report about me,

The trust, the position you gave me,

You must not only take it away, but also punish me severely,

Even if it costs me my life.

DUKE:

Bring Desdemona here.

OTHELLO:

Assistant, guide them, you know the place well.

Exit Iago and Attendants.

In the meantime, respectfully,

Let me tell you

How my relationship with this wonderful woman grew,

And how she loved me in return.

DUKE:

Go ahead, Othello.

OTHELLO:

Her father liked me and often invited me over.

Again and again, he wanted to hear the story of my life,

From childhood to adulthood. I talked of the battles, challenges, and victories

That I have experienced.

I told him everything.

I spoke of danger, battle, travel, and

Narrow escapes from deadly situations.

Like being captured and sold into slavery and my achieving freedom.

I spoke of vast caves, empty deserts,

Rugged mountain quarries, and hills reaching the sky.

I even talked about the tribes that eat each other,

The headhunters, and men who have faces on their chests.

When Desdemona heard these stories, she would sit captivated.

And if she had been pulled away to go do something

She finished as fast as she could so she could return and listen.

I took advantage of a moment when

She asked me to tell her more about my adventures.

She had heard bits and pieces of my tales,

But not fully, not with all her heart. I agreed,

And sometimes the stories made her sad.

After I finished my tale, she sighed in amazement.

She promised, in truth, that it was all sad, odd, and almost unbelievable.

She wished she hadn't heard it, yet at the same time, she wished

That heaven had made her into a man like me. She thanked me,

And told me, if I had a friend who loved her,

I should teach him to tell my story,

And that would win her over. It was on this suggestion that I acted.

She seemed to love me for the hardships I had survived,

And I loved her because she felt sorry for them.

This is the only trick I have used.

Here comes the lady. She can confirm this.

Desdemona, Iago, and assistants enter.

DUKE:

I believe this story could win my daughter over as well.

Good Brabantio,

Handle this issue as best you can.

BRABANTIO:

I beg you, let her speak.

If she admits that she was the one pursuing,

I'd be doomed.—Come here, kind daughter.

Of all these people, can you tell who you are most loyal to?

DESDEMONA:

My respected father,

I see my loyalty here is split.

To you, I owe my life and upbringing.

I respect you.

You are in a position of authority,

I am your daughter to this point. However, here's my husband.

Just as my mother respected you more than her own father,

I respect Othello, my new husband.

BRABANTIO:

May God be with you! I've made my peace with the situation.

Please, can we focus on state affairs now?

I'm heartbroken now. Come here, Othello.

I give you my daughter's hand with all my heart.

If it were up to me, I'd keep her away from you,

But that's not the case.

Honey, it's a good thing you're my only child.

If I had more, I'd probably be much to hard on them after this.

I'm done speaking, my Lord.

DUKE:

Let me speak honestly,
And provide a view that might
Help everyone accept these two as a couple.
Once a situation is final, the grief ends.
Hoping for a different outcome only leads to more pain.
Feeling sad over the past only invites new trouble.
A person robbed who can still smile steals
Something back from the thief.
On the other hand,
A person who is sad over a hopeless cause only robs himself.

BRABANTIO:

If the Turks were to invade Cyprus,
We wouldn't truly lose as long as we keep our spirits up.
A person handles punishment better when he accepts it.
It is much worse if he stays sad over his punishment.
But if he is both,
He's borrowing from his own comfort to pay for his sadness.
These sentences— whether they're taken sweetly or bitterly—
Are hard to explain when you're dealing with strong emotions.
But words are just words.
All I'm asking is that we move on with our business.

DUKE:

The Turks are preparing a strong force to attack Cyprus.
Othello, you're the one who knows the area best.
We have a reliable person there in command.
Yet, people say you're better for this job.

OTHELLO:

Respectable senators, I am tough
And comfortable in the face of warfare.
I will agree to go. I have one request:
I ask that my wife is given proper living arrangements
And respect that match her upbringing.

DUKE:

If you're okay with it,

She can stay with her father.

BRABANTIO:

I don't approve of that idea.

OTHELLO:

Neither do I.

DESDEMONA:

Neither do I.

I don't want to cause my father unnecessary worry by living

Under his watch.

Kind Duke, please listen to my words,

And support my simple request.

DUKE:

What do you want, Desdemona?

DESDEMONA:

I want to live with the man that I love, Othello.

Let the world know that

My heart is as committed as my husband's.

I saw Othello's kindness and courage,

And dedicated my life and fate to him.

So, dear leaders, if I'm left here,

A symbol of peace, while he goes to war,

The reasons I love him are taken from me,

And I will be sadden by his absence. Let me go with him.

OTHELLO:

Let her speak.

I pray to heaven, that I am not seeking this

For my own desires,

But to honor and respect her wishes.

Do not think I will neglect my duties

Because she is with me. No, no distractions

Caused by love will interfere with my duties,

And corrupt my mission.

DUKE:

Decide in private,

Whether she stays or goes.

We have other things to discuss and must act quickly.

FIRST SENATOR:

You need to leave tonight.

OTHELLO:

With all my heart.

DUKE:

We'll meet again here at nine in the morning.

Othello, choose an officer who can receive messages.

We will tell him our commands and he'll deliver them to you.

OTHELLO:

If it pleases your grace, my assistant,

A man of honesty and trust,

Will take care of my wife,

With anything else you think is necessary to send after me.

DUKE:

Let it be that way.

Good night to everyone. *[To Brabantio.]* And, noble father,

If goodness makes beauty even more beautiful,

Your son-in-law is more kind than cruel.

FIRST SENATOR:

Goodbye, brave Othello. Treat Desdemona well.

BRABANTIO:

Watch out for her, Othello.

She's tricked her father, and she may trick you.

Exit Duke, Senators, Officers, and others.

OTHELLO:

I trust her with my life! Honest Iago,

I have to leave my Desdemona to you.

Please, let your wife take good care of her,

And have them follow me at a safe time.

Come, Desdemona, I have only an hour

To spend with you.

Exit Othello and Desdemona.

RODERIGO:

Iago—

IAGO:

What's on your mind, good friend?

RODERIGO:

What should I do, do you think?

IAGO:

Why, go to bed and sleep.

RODERIGO:

I feel like drowning myself.

IAGO:

If you do, I won't be able to love you after. Such a silly gentleman!

RODERIGO:

It is silly to live when life is painful! Sometimes death is our only option.

IAGO:

How awful! I have lived in the world for four times seven years, and I could tell the difference between a good and a bad thing. I have never met a man who knew how to love himself. I'd rather act like a fool than drown myself over a woman.

RODERIGO:

What should I do? I admit it's embarrassing to have such a crush, but I can't help it.

IAGO:

Nonsense! It's within ourselves to be one way or another. Our bodies are gardens, and our thoughts and choices are the gardeners. So, if we decide to make a garden filled with a single type of plant or mix it with many, we are in control of what we do. We have the ability to balance.

RODERIGO:

That's not true.

IAGO:

All it is, is a feeling of strong desire and letting your will control you. Come on, act like a man. You're going to drown yourself? I've always been a good friend to you. Now more than ever, I can help you. Just put some money aside. Follow the wars and change your look. Trust me. It's not likely that Desdemona will love Othello forever, nor will he always love her. Their love started really strong but you'll see it won't last. Again, just save some money. The Moors are known for changing their minds. Fill your pocket with money. The things he now finds to be so sweet, he'll soon find bitter. She'll desire to be with someone her own age. When she's had enough of him, she'll realize her mistake. So, put some money aside. Instead of drowning, think about being happy with her.

RODERIGO:

Can I trust these words?

IAGO:

You can trust me. Go, make as much money as you can. I've told you over and over, I can't stand the Moor. My hatred is strong and yours is too. Let's join forces in our revenge against him. There are many things waiting to happen in the future. Start moving, go, gather your wealth. We'll talk more about this tomorrow. Goodbye.

RODERIGO:

Where will we meet in the morning?

IAGO:

At my place.

RODERIGO:

I'll be there early.

IAGO:

Goodbye. And do you understand me, Roderigo?

RODERIGO:

About what?

IAGO:

No more talk of drowning?

RODERIGO:

I have a new outlook. I'll sell what I have so I can save money.

Exit.

IAGO:

So I continue to profit from my fool, Roderigo.
I'd be wasting my talents spending time with him
If I wasn't able to get something out of it. I despise the Moor,
And rumor has it that he's had a romantic relationship with my
wife.
I don't know if it's true,
But just the suspicion of it is enough
For me to act as though it is. He trusts me,
Which will help me carry out my plan.
Cassio is a handsome man. However, I can
Take his position through trickery. Let me think!
After a while, I'll whisper in Othello's ear
That Cassio is too close with Desdemona.
He's very charming and easy to suspect, so it works.
The Moor is too trusting,
But he is also suspicious of others.
25 He can be led in a direction,
Just like a donkey.
I've got it. The plan is made. The darkest parts of night and hell
Must help bring this terrible plot to light for all to see.

Exit.

ACT II

SCENE 1. A SEAPORT IN CYPRUS. A PLATFORM

 [*Enter Montano and two gentlemen.*]

MONTANO:

What can you see from the coast?

FIRST GENTLEMAN:

Nothing. The sea is very wild.

I can't see any sails between the sea and the sky.

MONTANO:

The wind seems to be so violent on the land.

If it's this strong at sea, can any wooden ship withstand it?

What's happening out there?

SECOND GENTLEMAN:

The Turkish fleet is sailing apart.

If you stand by the seashore,

It's like the angry waves are throwing water up at the clouds,

Trying to put out the bright stars in the sky.

I have never seen such a stormy sea.

MONTANO:

If the Turkish ships are not in a safe place,

They must be sinking.

It's impossible for them to survive this.

Enter a Third Gentleman.

THIRD GENTLEMAN:

Hey, guys! The fight is over.

The terrible storm has beaten the Turks

So badly that they had to stop their plans.

A brave Venetian ship has seen the Turks' fleet mostly ruined.

MONTANO:

Really? Are you sure?

THIRD GENTLEMAN:

Yes, the Venetian ship has arrived here.

Michael Cassio, who works for the mighty Othello, is here.

Othello is at sea and has full power here in Cyprus.

MONTANO:

I'm pleased to hear it. He is a worthy leader.

THIRD GENTLEMAN:

However, this same Cassio, even as he comforts us

With the news of the Turks' defeat, appears very tired.

He prays for Othello's safety since they were separated

In a terrible and violent storm.

MONTANO:

I pray to the heavens he is safe.

He's an excellent leader.

Come on, let's head to the seashore!

We can watch the ship that has just arrived.

We can stay on the look out for brave Othello.

THIRD GENTLEMAN:

Let's go! There will be more arrivals every minute.

Enter Cassio.

CASSIO:

Thank you, the brave people of this war-like island

for praising Othello! Oh, may the heavens

Protect him! I lost sight of him in a treacherous sea.

MONTANO:

Is his ship in good condition?

CASSIO:

His ship is solidly built and his navigator

Is very skilled and experienced.

Therefore, I'm worried,

But still confident in him.

From somewhere, a shout, "A sail, a sail, a sail!"

A Messenger enters.

CASSIO:

What's that noise?

MESSENGER:

The town is deserted. At the edge of the sea

Groups of people stand, shouting, "A sail!"

CASSIO:

My hopes are that it is our governor, Othello.

A gunshot.

SECOND GENTLEMAN:

They're firing their guns as a mark of respect.

It must be our friends!

CASSIO:

Please, sir, go find out,

And tell us who exactly has arrived.

SECOND GENTLEMAN:

I will.

He exits.

MONTANO:

So, good lieutenant, is your general married?

CASSIO:

Luck is on our side, he's got a wife

Who is beyond description and praise.

She outshines even the finest words

And stands out in the world

More than anyone else.

Enter Second Gentleman.

What's the news? Who has arrived?

SECOND GENTLEMAN:

It's Iago, assistant to the general.

CASSIO:

He had a quick and safe journey.

Even the storms, huge waves, and strong winds,

The deadly rocks, and shifting sands,

Let them pass safely,

In honor of the wonderful Desdemona.

MONTANO:

Who is she?

CASSIO:

She's the woman I mentioned, the wife of our general.

Iago is caring for her.

He got here a whole week ahead of schedule.

Oh-- may God protect Othello

So he can join us soon, safe in Desdemona's arms,

Cheering up all of us on this island!

Enter Desdemona, Iago, Roderigo, and Emilia.

Wow! The most important person from the ship is on land!

People of Cyprus, respect her.

Welcome, lady! May God's grace be with you,

In front of you, behind you, and all around you!

DESDEMONA:

Thank you, brave Cassio.

What news do you have of my husband?

CASSIO:

He hasn't arrived yet, but I do know

That he's safe and will be here soon.

DESDEMONA:

29 O, but I worry — how did you lose each other?

[Within.] A sail, a sail!

CASSIO:

The huge struggle between the ocean and skies
Separated our group. But, listen! A ship.

Guns sound off within.

SECOND GENTLEMAN:

They're saying there's an arrival to the fortress.
This ship is a friend, as well.

CASSIO:

Check for any news.

Exit Gentleman.

Good sir, you are welcome. *[To Emilia.]* Welcome, lady.
I hope you don't mind, good Iago,
That I'm being polite. It's just how I was raised
And why I'm openly courteous.

Kissing her cheek.

IAGO:

Sir, if she gave you as much of her lips
As she often uses her tongue on me,
You would have enough.

DESDEMONA:

Sadly, she doesn't say much.

IAGO:

In truth, she says too much.
I notice it most when I want to sleep.
However, in front of you, lady, I admit,
She speaks a bit from her heart,
And scolds with her thoughts.

EMILIA:

You don't really have a reason to say that.

IAGO:

Alright, alright. You women are like paintings outdoors,
Bells in your living rooms, wild-cats in your kitchens,
Saints when you're wronged, devils when you're upset,

Actors in your house chores, and housewives in your beds.
DESDEMONA:
Oh, quiet down, you liar!
IAGO:
Nope, it's true, otherwise I'm not who I say I am.
You wake up to have fun, and go to bed to work.
EMILIA:
You aren't going to write my praise.
IAGO:
No, I won't.
DESDEMONA:
What would you say about me, if you were to praise me?
IAGO:
Oh kind lady, don't make me,
Because I can be quite harsh.
DESDEMONA:
Let's test this. Has someone gone to the harbor?
IAGO:
Yes.
DESDEMONA:
I am not happy, but I do pretend
To be something I'm not, by appearing different.—
So, how would you compliment me?
IAGO:
Honestly, my creativity
Comes from my head very slowly,
Here's what it produces:
If a lady is pretty and smart,
One is for use, the other uses it.
DESDEMONA:
Well complimented! What if she's dark-skinned and witty?
IAGO:
If she is dark-skinned and clever,
She'll find a fair partner who will suit her.

DESDEMONA:

That's even worse.

EMILIA:

What if she's beautiful and foolish?

IAGO:

Nobody who was beautiful has ever been foolish.

Even her silly moments helped her win a partner.

DESDEMONA:

These are old silly contradictions to make fools laugh at the bar. What pitiful compliment do you have for a woman who's unattractive and foolish?

IAGO:

Nobody so unattractive and foolish exists,

Who doesn't do foolish things that beautiful and smart ones do.

DESDEMONA:

Oh, riddler! You compliment the worst, the best. But what compliment could you give to a truly deserving woman, one who has earned respect on her own merits?

IAGO:

A woman who was always beautiful and never mean,

Could speak her mind and yet was never loud,

Never lacked money and yet was never showy,

Controlled her desires, yet knew when she could get things she wanted.

A woman who, when angered, prepares her revenge,

She, who had control over her emotions.

She, who was never weak in wisdom.

She was like no other, if there ever was such a girl!

DESDEMONA:

To do what exactly?

IAGO:

To raise children and be a housewife.

DESDEMONA:

What a worn-out and weak ending!—Don't listen to him, Emilia,

Even if he's your husband. What do you think, Cassio?
Isn't he random and ill-mannered?

CASSIO:

He is direct, ma'am.
You might appreciate him more as a soldier than a scholar.

IAGO:

[*Quietly to himself.*] He takes her hand. Keep talking, whisper. With this simple plan, I'll catch a big fish like Cassio. Keep smiling at her, sure. I will trap you in your own actions. That's right, it's happening. If this trick gets you removed from being my lieutenant, then you probably shouldn't have kissed your fingers so often, since it looks like you are ready to do it again. Good job! Well done, a sweet greeting! Yes, it's happening. Are you putting your fingers to your lips again? I wish they were fingers to cover your mouth and silence you for your own good!

Trumpets playing.

It's Othello! I recognize his trumpet.

CASSIO:

That's the truth.

DESDEMONA:

Let's welcome him.

CASSIO:

Look, here he comes!

Enter Othello and others.

OTHELLO:

Oh, my brave fighter!

DESDEMONA:

My Othello!

OTHELLO:

It brings me as much amazement as it brings joy.
Oh, the joy in my soul!
If after every storm comes such peace,
May the winds blow until they stir death from his sleep!
If I should die now, I would be most at peace.

My soul is so happy,

It can't be replaced by any other comfort.

DESDEMONA:

May the heavens never allow our love

And joy to do anything but grow

As our days do!

OTHELLO:

Amen to that, divine powers!

I can't possibly express how happy I am.

This feeling stops me in my tracks. It's overwhelming:

And this, and this, the greatest disagreements will be *[They kiss.]*

That our hearts ever create!

IAGO:

[Aside.] Oh, you are in harmony now,

But I'll adjust the strings that create this music,

As honest as I am.

OTHELLO:

Let's head to the castle.—

News, friends, our battles are over, the Turks are gone.

What's the word on my old acquaintances?

Honey, you will be well liked in Cyprus.

I've found great love among them. Oh, my dearest,

I'm going on and on.—Please, good Iago,

Go to the bay and unload my chests.

Bring the master to the fortress.

He is reliable.—Come, Desdemona,

Nice to see you again in Cyprus.

Exit Othello, Desdemona, and Attendants.

IAGO:

33 Meet me soon at the harbor. Come here. If you're brave—as it is said, average men in love become noble, more than they naturally are. Listen to me. The lieutenant is on guard duty tonight. First, I must tell you this: Desdemona is completely in love with him.

RODERIGO:

With him? That's not possible, man.

IAGO:

Pay attention to this, and open your mind to what I'm saying. Remember the passion that made her fall for the Moor because of his stories. Do you think she'll keep loving him just because he can talk a lot? Don't be naive. She needs more. What joy can she have staring at someone so different? When the thrill of their love has settled, there should be sparks like shared interests, similar age, matching manners, and physical beauty. All these are areas where the Moor falls short. Because he lacks these qualities, she's going to quickly realize she's made a mistake and she'll start feeling annoyed and fed up with Othello. This will push her to find someone new. Now, considering all of this, who better fits this opportunity than Cassio? He's a smooth talker who only cares about looking good and civilized in order to hide his mischievous and uncontrolled desires. Indeed, there's no one else! He's smooth and an expert at finding opportunities. He's a crafty trickster. Moreover, he's handsome, youthful, and a full-blown charmer. The lady has already noticed him.

RODERIGO:

I'm struggling to view her as a virtuous person.

IAGO:

Oh, please! If she were really so good, she wouldn't have fallen in love with the Moor. Give me a break! Didn't you see her holding hands with Cassio? Didn't you notice that?

RODERIGO:

Yes, I did see that. But I thought it was just politeness.

IAGO:

No, it's more than that, I promise you. It's a clear hint at romance. Their faces were so close that their breaths were almost one. Evil thoughts, Roderigo! She's giving him the signals and messages to advance. Now listen to me, as I'm the one who got you all the way from Venice. Keep an eye on them tonight. I will give you the commands. And don't worry, Cassio doesn't know you. I'll stay close by. Find a way to push Cassio into anger.

RODERIGO:

Alright. I'm in.

IAGO:

Listen, he has a temper. Any fighting could spark so much unrest among the people of Cyprus that they'll demand Cassio's removal. You'll be closer to you'll go and we'll be near success.

RODERIGO:

I'll do this if the right chance presents itself.

IAGO:

You can do it. Meet me later near the fort. I must bring his belongings from the ship. Goodbye.

RODERIGO:

Goodbye.

Exit.

IAGO:

I am quite confident that Cassio is in love with her.

It's likely that she loves him back.

The Moor, despite my dislike for him,

Is consistently kind, loving, and noble.

I believe he could be a great match for Desdemona.

Now that the charming Moor has slipped into the place I wish to be.

This bothers at me too.

Nothing will make me happy until I've had my revenge,

Until we are equally hurt, in terms of love and loss,

Or, if not, to stir such deep jealousy in the Moor

That nothing will make him happy. To accomplish this,

This fool from Venice, who I consider worthless, will be important.

Let him start hunting and watch as the plan unfolds.

I've got this 'Michael Cassio' precisely where I want him,

And I am going to make him look like a bad guy to the Moor.

I will make the Moor so grateful, he will shower me with love.

Yet I'll be making a fool of him all along. I'll make him go crazy.
The plan is here.
The face of betrayal is never known until it's used.

Exit.

SCENE 11. A STREET

38 *[OTHELLO'S HERALD (MESSENGER) ENTERS WITH AN ANNOUNCEMENT.]*

HERALD:

Othello, our brave and honorable leader, wants everyone to know some great news. He has just learned that the Turkish fleet has been totally destroyed! He wants everyone to celebrate in whatever way they want. Some might dance, some might start bonfires. Everyone should have fun. On top of this fantastic news, it's also the day of his wedding. Businesses should be closed and everyone is free to start partying from 5:00PM to 11:00PM. God bless the island of Cyprus and our great leader, Othello!

Exit.

SCENE III. A HALL IN THE CASTLE

39 *[ENTER OTHELLO, DESDEMONA, CASSIO AND THEIR HELPERS.]*

OTHELLO:
Good Michael Cassio, watch the guard tonight.
Make sure you have self-control and don't party too hard.
CASSIO:
Iago has directions, but I'll make sure everything's taken care of.
OTHELLO:
Iago is very honest. Good night Michael.
Let me talk to you early tomorrow.
[To Desdemona.]
Now my love, we have good times to look forward to.
Good night.

Othello, Desdemona and their helpers leave. Enter Iago.
CASSIO:
Welcome, Iago. We need to go to our guard duty.
IAGO:
Not yet, lieutenant. It's not even ten o'clock. Othello sent us on

duty early because he wishes to go to bed with Desdemona. Let's not blame him. He hasn't spent enough time with her and he loves her.

CASSIO:

She is truly amazing.

IAGO:

And, believe me, she's full of spirit.

CASSIO:

Yes, she's really quite a lady.

IAGO:

What great eyes she has! They almost invite people to flirt with her.

CASSIO:

Her eyes are truly inviting. However, she's proper.

IAGO:

And when she talks, isn't it like a love song?

CASSIO:

She is indeed perfect.

IAGO:

Well, come lieutenant. I have a pot of wine and outside are two Cypriot gentlemen who want a toast to Othello.

CASSIO:

Not tonight, good Iago. I really don't handle alcohol well. I wish there were another way to have fun.

IAGO:

Oh, they are our friends. Just have one glass! I'll drink for you.

CASSIO:

I have already had one drink tonight, and that was weak, and look, how it affects me. I am weak when it comes to drinking, and I dare not risk my weakness with any more.

IAGO:

What? It's a night of celebration! The gentlemen are asking.

CASSIO:

Where are they?

IAGO:

They're at the door. Please, invite them in.

CASSIO:

I'll do it, but I do not like this.

Exit.

IAGO:

If I can get him to have just one more drink,

With what he has drunk tonight already,

He'll be as argumentative and offensive as a dog.

Now, my lovesick fool Roderigo,

Whose love for Desdemona has turned him almost inside out,

Has made a toast to Desdemona. Cassio's on guard duty.

Three men of Cyprus, noble and ready to take action,

That hold their honors dearly,

Have I messed up with drinking,

And they're on guard duty too. Now, among this group of drunks,

I will get our Cassio involved in something

That may upset the island. But here they come:

If things go according to my plan,

It's all smooth sailing from here.

Cassio, Montano and the gentlemen enter, followed by a servant carrying wine.

CASSIO:

Oh man, I'm already feeling the effects of this wine.

MONTANO:

It's still early, my friend. You've not enough. Considering you're a soldier...

IAGO:

Bring on the wine!

Sings.

Listen to the clink of glasses, clink, clink,

    Let's hear those glasses clink!

    A soldier is a man,

    Life is short,

So why not let a soldier drink?

A round of wine, fellows!

CASSIO:

What a splendid song.

IAGO:

I picked it up in England, where they sure know how to hold their drinks. Your Danes, Germans, even the huge Hollander—drink up, fellas!—they've got nothing on your English.

CASSIO:

Are the English so skilled in their drinking?

IAGO:

Indeed, they out-drink everyone. They can have your Dane unconscious at the table. They can overpower your German without breaking a sweat, make your Hollander throw up even before the next round is ready.

CASSIO:

Let's drink to the health of our leader!

MONTANO:

I'm in agreement, lieutenant! I'll match you drink for drink!

IAGO:

Ah, wonderful England!

Sings.

King Stephen was a fine man,
> *His pants only cost him a buck.*
> *He thought they were still too pricey,*
> *And he told the tailor he was out of luck!*
> *He was a man who was well-known,*
> *And you, sir, are a nobody.*
> *Pride is what brings a country down,*
> *So wrap your old cloak around your body.*

More wine, fellows!?

CASSIO:

Wow! This song is even more delightful than the previous one.

IAGO:

Want to hear it once more?

CASSIO:

No, I believe someone who acts like that doesn't deserve his position.

But remember, God will make the final judgement.

There are some souls who will be saved, and some that won't.

IAGO:

That's right, good lieutenant.

CASSIO:

Given my own way, I wouldn't upset the general or anyone else of higher rank. I just hope to be saved too.

IAGO:

I hope the same for me, lieutenant.

CASSIO:

Yes, but if you don't mind my saying, I should be saved before you since I'm the lieutenant. But let's stop this type of talk and focus on our work. We have to ask for forgiveness for our sins! Gentlemen, let's pay attention to our duties. And please, don't think I'm drunk. This is Iago, my second in command. This is my right hand and this is my left. I'm not drunk. I can stand straight and talk clearly.

ALL:

You're doing great.

CASSIO:

Well, then maybe I don't seem so drunk.

Exit.

MONTANO:

Let's go on our watch now.

IAGO:

You see that guy who just left,

He's a great soldier, good enough to act alongside Caesar.

But you need to see his weakness too,

They're equally balanced with his strengths.

He's quite the character and drinker.

I worry the trust Othello gives him during this mission

Might cause trouble.

MONTANO:

Does he get drunk often?

IAGO:

He always does this before he sleeps.

He would probably double his watch duties

If it wasn't for his heavy drinking that puts him to sleep each

night.

MONTANO:

It could be a good idea to remind the general about this.

Perhaps he doesn't see it, or his good nature

Values the good qualities he sees in Cassio

Make him unable to see his wrongs.

Do you think I should say something?

Enter Roderigo.

IAGO:

(Whispers to Roderigo.) Hey, Roderigo!

Please, go after Lieutenant Cassio.

Exit Roderigo.

MONTANO:

It's really such a shame.

The noble Moor risks so much by trusting someone,

As his second in command,

Who's got such obvious flaws.

It would be a good thing to tell Othello,

If someone were to do so.

IAGO:

I see, but I would also never cause trouble

And upset the peace in this beautiful island.

As much as I like Cassio and would like to help him,

That's not my place. But, wait! Do you hear something?

*There's a cry from off stage: "Help! Help!" Cassio enters,
driving Roderigo in front of him.*

CASSIO:

You scoundrel! You good-for-nothing!

MONTANO:

What's the problem, Lieutenant?

CASSIO:

Should a lowlife like you teach me how to do my duty?

I can break you into a million pieces!

RODERIGO:

Are you threatening me?

CASSIO:

What, are you speaking of, rascal?

He hits Roderigo.

MONTANO:

Easy there, Lieutenant. Please, I beg you, hold back!

CASSIO:

Let go of me, sir, or you're the next to get hit!

MONTANO:

Calm down, you're intoxicated.

CASSIO:

Drunk?

They start fighting.

IAGO:

[Whispers to Roderigo.] Run! Shout out that there's chaos here.

Roderigo exits.

No no, dear Lieutenant.

All in good faith, gentlemen. Help!

Here, we need help!

Look at what a ruckus this is, during our night watch!

A bell starts ringing.

Who's ringing that bell?

In all likelihood, the whole town will wake!

Lieutenant, you must stop,

Or you risk shame and ridicule forever.

> *Othello and his attendants enter.*

OTHELLO:

What's going on here?

MONTANO:

Yikes, I'm still bleeding, I'm badly hurt.

OTHELLO:

Everyone, stop! For your own safety, stop!

IAGO:

Wait a minute! Have you all lost your senses?

Listen! Othello is speaking to you! Stop, stop!

OTHELLO:

What's going on, everyone? Where did this come from?

Have we turned into bullies and enemies?

Whoever continues fighting loses respect.

What's the problem, everyone?

Iago, you look sad, talk to me. Who started this? I insist, tell me.

IAGO:

I don't know. Just minutes ago, everyone was friends,

Getting along as if they were a bride and groom

Ready to share a bed; and then, out of the blue,

As if some strange force took over,

Swords were drawn, and they started attacking each other,

Becoming bloody enemies. I can't say

How this silly fight started.

I just wish I hadn't been part of it!

OTHELLO:

How did you end up in this mess, Michael?

CASSIO:

I beg your pardon. I can't talk about it just yet.

OTHELLO:

Montano, you're usually a good person.

Your calmness is known far and wide.

So what's going on?

Why are you ruining your good name,
And wasting your valuable reputation?
45 Can a troublemaker really be responsible for this?
Answer me that.

MONTANO:

Respected Othello, I'm seriously wounded.
Your officer, Iago, can tell you about it,
While I rest my voice, which is hurting me now,
I'll tell you everything that I know.
I can't recall anything I've done wrong tonight,
Unless it's a crime to protect myself.

OTHELLO:

Now, I'm getting angry.
Tell me,
How did this terrible brawl start, who caused it,
And anyone who is found guilty in this matter,
No matter how close he is to me, will lose my trust.
Is it right, in a town at war,
Where people are already so scared,
To stir up more fighting?
This is outrageous. Iago, who started it all?

MONTANO:

If you're biased or abusing your position,
And you tell anything other than the truth,
Then you're no soldier.

IAGO:

Don't accuse me of that.
I would rather cut my own tongue out
Than say anything that might hurt Michael Cassio.
I believe that telling the truth
Won't harm him. This is what happened, General:
While I was talking to Montano,
A man came running, yelling for help,
And Cassio charged at him with his sword,

Ready to strike. Sir, this man
Enters to stop Cassio and asks him to pause.
I chose to chase after the yelling man,
In case his noise (as it happened)
Might scare the town.
He got away from me and then I heard the sound and falling of
swords.
When I came back, I found them
Fighting fiercely, just like they were
When you separate them.
I can't report more about this issue.
All men make mistakes.
Although Cassio did a slight wrong to him,
I believe that Cassio,
Received some strange unfair treatment,
Which no one could stand for.

OTHELLO:

I know, Iago,
Your honesty and loyalty lessen this issue,
Making it seem not so bad for Cassio. Cassio, I care for you,
But you can no longer be my officer.

Enter Desdemona, with helpers.

Look, my gentle love is upset!

DESDEMONA:

What's going on?

OTHELLO:

Everything's fine now, darling. Let's go to bed.
Sir, for your injuries, I will be your doctor.
Lead him off.

Montano is led off.

Iago, carefully look around the town
And calm everyone down.
Come, Desdemona. It's a soldier's life
To have their peaceful sleep disturbed by conflict.

Everyone leaves except for Iago and Cassio.

IAGO:

What, are you hurt, lieutenant?

CASSIO:

Yes, beyond all surgery.

IAGO:

Heaven forbid!

CASSIO:

My good name, my good name, my good name! Oh, I've lost my good name! I've lost the most important part of me. My good name, Iago, my good name!

IAGO:

Well, I'm an honest man, and I thought you were physically hurt, which would've made more sense than worrying about your reputation. Reputation is a tricky and can change in an instant. You haven't lost any reputation unless you believe you're a loser. Look, there are ways to get back in good standing with Othello. He's angry now, but apologize to him again, and he'll forgive you.

CASSIO:

I'd rather be hated than to disappoint such a good leader with such a reckless and drunken behavior. Drunk? Talk nonsense? Fight? Show off? Curse? And have meaningless discussions with my own shadow? Oh, you invisible spirit of wine, if you have no other name, we should call you devil!

IAGO:

Who was the man you went after with your sword? What had he done to you?

CASSIO:

I don't remember.

IAGO:

Is it really true?

CASSIO:

I remember bits and pieces, but not clearly. Wine is a real enemy that robs us of our good sense!

IAGO:

Why, you seem alright now. How did you manage to sober up?

CASSIO:

The demon of drinking made way for the demon of anger. One mistake just leads to another, making me truly hate myself.

IAGO:

Come on, you're being too hard on yourself. Considering the time, the place, and the situation, I wish this hadn't happened. Since it has, fix it for your own good.

CASSIO:

I will ask him for my job back, but now he thinks I'm a drunk! Even if I had as many mouths as a monster, such a response would shut them all up. To be sensible one minute, a fool the next, and then a beast! How strange!

IAGO:

Come on, come on, good wine can be a great companion, if used properly. Don't protest against it anymore. And, good lieutenant, I believe you know I care about you.

CASSIO:

You're right, I can see that, sir—I was drunk!

IAGO:

You, or any guy, could get drunk once in a while, man. Here's what you should do. Our leader's wife is the real boss now. The leader's given himself over to admiring, observing, and being amazed by her qualities and beauty. Just talk honestly to her. Ask for her help to get your position back. She's so generous, so nice, so skillful, and so good-natured, and she thinks it's wrong not to do more than people ask of her. With this conflict between you and her husband, try asking her to patch it up. And I bet anything, your relationship with him will end up stronger than it was before.

CASSIO:

Nice advice.

IAGO:

I swear, I'm just trying to help in the most genuine way.

CASSIO:

I'll think about it. Early tomorrow morning, I'll go to the good-hearted Desdemona for help. If things don't change, I'm completely out of luck.

IAGO:

You're thinking clearly. Good night, boss, I gotta do my rounds.

CASSIO:

Good night, trustworthy Iago.

Exit.

IAGO:

So, who's going to accuse me of being a bad guy?

Is my advice not sensible and honest?

I'm am being honest about how to get on Othello's good side again.

It's easy to get Desdemona on board

For any decent cause. She's as gentle and giving

As Mother Nature herself. And she'll be able to persuade

Othello to join in to proves just how much he loves her.

She has the power to make, unmake, and do as she pleases.

Am I then, a villain

For telling Cassio to use the same strategy for his own benefit?

I look like an angel, but I have devil goals.

When this honest fool

Asks Desdemona to fix everything,

And she advocates passionately to the Moor,

I'll introduce a harmful thought into his ear.

I'll make him think she only wants him back to satisfy her desires.

The more she tries to help him,

The more she risks damaging her reputation with the Moor.

I will transform her good intentions into a trap,

And use her kindness to trick them all.

Enter Roderigo.

What's the matter, Roderigo?

RODERIGO:

I'm just keeping up in the chase not like the hunter, but more like an observer. I've almost spent all my money, I got messed up pretty bad tonight and I think the end result will be nothing. Then, with no money and a bit more wisdom, I'll have to go back to Venice.

IAGO:

Those who lack patience are truly poor!

Has there ever been a wound that healed instantly?

You know we operate using brains, not magic spells.

Look at our progress though!

With one small act, you've got Cassio fired.

Wait out your time for a bit.

Having fun and being busy make time fly by.

Go rest and head to the place you're supposed to be.

I'll tell you more later.

No, really, get going.

Roderigo exits.

There are two things I need to do,

My wife needs to persuade her lady to support Cassio.

I'll push her towards that.

In the meantime, I'll draw the Moor away,

And get him to see Cassio

Spending time with his wife at the right moment. Yes, that's the plan.

Let's not dull our plan by being cold and late.

Iago exits.

ACT III

SCENE 1. CYPRUS. BEFORE THE CASTLE

 [CASSIO ENTERS WITH MUSICIANS AND A CLOWN.]

CASSIO:

Musicians, please play a short tune here, and say "Good morning, general" afterward.

Music plays. A clown enters.

CLOWN:

Why, musicians, were your instruments made in Naples, that they sound so nasally?

FIRST MUSICIAN:

What do you mean, sir?

CLOWN:

Are these wind instruments you're playing?

FIRST MUSICIAN:

Indeed, they are sir.

CLOWN:

Well, there's a story behind that.

FIRST MUSICIAN:

What kind of story, sir?

CLOWN:

Well, it involves many wind instruments I know. But listen, here's some money for you. It's from the general. He asks you out of kindness to stop the noise.

FIRST MUSICIAN:

Alright, sir, we'll stop.

CLOWN.

If you have any music that can't be heard, play it again. But I understand the general doesn't really enjoy music.

FIRST MUSICIAN.

We don't have any music like that, sir.

CLOWN:

Then put your instruments away, because I'm leaving. Go on, disappear!

The Musicians exit.

CASSIO:

Did you hear that, my honest friend?

CLOWN:

No, I didn't hear your honest friend. But I heard you.

CASSIO:

Please, stop with your clever remarks. Here's some gold for you: if the lady who helps the general's wife is awake, tell her Cassio wants a small talk. Can you do that?

CLOWN:

The lady is awake, sir.

If she will come here,

It will be my pleasure to let her know.

CASSIO:

Please do, my good friend.

Exit Clown. Enter Iago.

Good timing, Iago.

IAGO:

You haven't gone to bed, have you?

CASSIO:

No, I haven't. We said goodbye before sunrise.

I took a chance, Iago, and sent a message to your wife.

I'm asking her to help me talk to the noble Desdemona.

IAGO:

I'll send her your way soon.

I'll create a distraction to get the general out of the way

So that you can have some private discussion.

CASSIO:

I'm grateful for that.

Exit Iago.

I've never come across anyone from Florence

Who was as warm and honest.

Enter Emilia.

EMILIA:

Good Morning, good lieutenant.

I am sorry for your troubles,

But everything will indeed get better.

The general and his wife have discussed it,

And she's spoken up for you.

The General says that the person you offended

Is well-respected and related to some very important people

And that he couldn't just ignore what happened.

But he reassures that he still holds you in high regard,

And he would just prefer to choose a better moment to reintro-
duce you.

CASSIO:

Still, I plead with you,

If you think it's okay or that it can be done,

Allow me a chance to speak briefly with Desdemona alone.

EMILIA:

Please come in.

I'll ensure you're placed where you can talk freely with her.
CASSIO:
I am very grateful to you.

Exit.

SCENE 11. CYPRUS. A ROOM IN THE CASTLE

[Enter Othello, Iago, and some gentlemen.]

OTHELLO:

Iago, give these letters to the ship's captain.

He'll take them to the senate for me.

Once that's done, I'll be going for a walk.

Come and find me there.

IAGO:

Of course, sir. I'll do it.

OTHELLO:

Gentlemen, shall we check on the fortress?

GENTLEMEN:

We'll follow your lead, sir.

Exit.

SCENE III. CYPRUS. THE GARDEN OF THE CASTLE

 [DESDEMONA, CASSIO AND EMILIA WALK IN.]

DESDEMONA:

Be sure, dear Cassio,

I will do everything I can to help.

EMILIA:

Please do, madam.

I can guarantee this upsets my husband

Just like it was his own problem.

DESDEMONA:

He truly is fair. Don't worry, Cassio.

I will make sure you and my husband restore things.

CASSIO:

Thank you, madam.

No matter what happens to me,

I will always be devoted to you.

DESDEMONA:

I am aware. Thank you.

You do love my husband.

You've known him for a long time.

Be sure, he won't stay distant any longer.

CASSIO:

Yes, ma'am,

I worry he might forget about me.

DESDEMONA:

Don't worry about that.

Standing here with Emilia,

I promise you will keep your job.

I take my promises seriously

And I will talk to my husband until he runs out of patience.

Even his meals and sleep won't get in the way of your request.

So cheer up, Cassio!

I will not forget your cause.

Othello and Iago walk in.

EMILIA:

Madam, your husband is coming.

CASSIO:

Madam, I'll excuse myself now.

DESDEMONA:

Why, stay, and listen to what I have to say.

CASSIO:

I can't, madam. I'm not in a good state of mind,

Not fit for my own needs.

DESDEMONA:

All right, use your best judgement then.

Cassio exits.

IAGO:

Uh, I don't like the look of that.

OTHELLO:

What did you say?

IAGO:

Nothing much, my lord. I'm not sure.

OTHELLO:

Wasn't that Cassio leaving my wife?

IAGO:

Cassio? Surely not, my lord.

I don't think he would sneak off like that if he saw you coming.

OTHELLO:

I believe it was him though.

DESDEMONA:

How are you, my lord?

I was just speaking with someone.

A man who's upset because of you.

OTHELLO:

Who are you referring to?

DESDEMONA:

Why, your lieutenant, Cassio. Please, my lord,

Accept his apology.

If he doesn't really care about you,

Then I can't tell when someone is being genuine.

Please, ask him to come back.

OTHELLO:

Did he just leave?

DESDEMONA:

Yes, he was very kind.

But he has left part of his sadness with me

Please, ask him to return.

OTHELLO:

Not now, my dear Desdemona, some other time.

DESDEMONA:

But will it be soon?

OTHELLO:

The sooner, my dear, for you.

DESDEMONA:

Will it be tonight at dinner?

OTHELLO:

No, not tonight.
DESDEMONA:
Tomorrow at lunch, then?
OTHELLO:
I won't be home for lunch.
I have a meeting with the captains at the citadel.
DESDEMONA:
Then how about tomorrow night, or Tuesday morning,
On Tuesday noon, or Tuesday night or Wednesday morning.
Please set the time, but do not make it longer than
Three days. Truly, he's regretful.
Wars must teach lessons
From their best men. It seems hardly a fault
Worthy of a private scolding. When will he rejoin?
Tell me, Othello. I wonder,
What could you ask of me, that I would say no,
Or be so hesitant. What? Michael Cassio,
Has defended you so many times, so it's such a big deal
To get him back! Trust me, I could do much.
OTHELLO:
Please no more. Let him come whenever he wishes.
I won't deny you anything.
DESDEMONA:
Well, this is not a big favor.
It's as if I were asking you to wear your gloves,
Or eat certain food, or to keep warm,
Or asking you to do something good
For your own health. But, when I need a favor
That really tests your love,
It will be a hard one, and hard to agree to.
OTHELLO:
I will not deny you anything.
But please grant me this one thing,
To let me have some time by myself.

DESDEMONA:
Why would I deny you? No, goodbye, my lord.
OTHELLO:
Goodbye, my Desdemona. I'll come straight to you.
DESDEMONA:
Emilia, come. Do as you wish.
Whatever happens, I am obedient.
Desdemona exits with Emilia.
OTHELLO:
Wonderful girl! But she may ruin my soul!
Yet I truly love her! And when I stop loving her,
There will be chaos.
IAGO:
My noble lord,

58 **OTHELLO:**
What did you say, Iago?
IAGO:
Did Michael Cassio, when you courted my lady,
Know about your love?
OTHELLO:
He did, from beginning to end. Why do you ask?
IAGO:
Just trying to clear my thoughts.
No more harm than that.
OTHELLO:
Why do you want to clear your thoughts, Iago?
IAGO:
I didn't think he knew about her.
OTHELLO:
Oh yes, he would communicate between us often.
IAGO:
Really?

OTHELLO:

Really? Yes, really. Do you see something wrong in that?

Isn't he a good fellow?

IAGO:

Good, my lord?

OTHELLO:

Good? Yes, good.

IAGO:

My lord, as far as I know.

OTHELLO:

What do you think?

IAGO:

Think, my lord?

OTHELLO:

Think, my lord? He's repeating me,

As if there was some monster in his thoughts

Too scary to be shown. You must mean something.

I heard you say just now, you "didn't like that,"

When Cassio left my wife. What didn't you like?

And when I told you he was part of my plan

When Desdemona and I first fell in love, you said, "Really?"

You looked worried.

As if you were hiding some nasty thoughts: if you love me,

Show me your thoughts.

IAGO:

My lord, you know I love you.

OTHELLO:

I think you do.

I know you're full of love and honesty.

Think about your words before you say them.

But I sense your earlier words are hints

About something troubling going on within.

Feelings shouldn't control us.

IAGO:

About Michael Cassio,
I am certain that he can be trusted.
OTHELLO:
I think he's trustworthy.
IAGO:
People should act how they say they will,
But it's sometimes hard to tell.
OTHELLO:
I wish people were genuine. Is he?
IAGO:
I believe Cassio is an honest man.
OTHELLO:
Wait, I still think there's more to this.
Please speak openly about your thoughts,
like you're just talking aloud to yourself, and let your darkest thoughts
Have the strongest words.
IAGO:
My good lord, forgive me.
Even though it's my job to serve you,
I'm not encouraged to share all my thoughts freely.
Especially when they might be ugly.
I also don't want to fill your mind with worry.
OTHELLO:
You're plotting against your friend, Iago,
If you believe he's been wrong but you're keeping your thoughts from him.
IAGO:
I beg you,
Even though I admit I can jump to negative conclusions,
It's a weakness of mine to make up things that aren't even there.
I ask that you ignore my guesses and not let them bother you.
Don't create extra worries based on me.
It would neither benefit you nor uphold my character

To share all my thoughts with you.
OTHELLO:
What are you trying to say?
IAGO:
A good reputation is a treasure of a person's soul.
If somebody steals my money, they've only taken trash.
It was mine, now it's his, but many have had it before.
However, if someone takes away my good reputation,
They've robbed me of something that can't help them,
But makes me truly poor.
OTHELLO:
Please. I need to know what you're thinking.
IAGO:
Even if my heart were in your hand,
You couldn't know, and won't as long as it's safely within me.
OTHELLO:
What?
IAGO:
Take care, my lord, of the creature called jealousy.
It's an ugly green-eyed monster
That makes fun of the food it feasts on.
When you know you're being tricked,
You can be happy because you won't be tricked again.
But, oh, what a horrible thing to doubt and suspect someone without
Knowing the truth!
OTHELLO:
Oh, it's a terrible feeling!
IAGO:
Someone who's poor
But content is rich indeed.
But the person who's wealthy
Without end but always fears poverty is poor.
May heavens protect all the people

I care about from jealousy!

OTHELLO:

Why, why is this happening?

Do you think I want to live a life filled with jealousy,

Always following moon phases with new doubts?

No. Once I've doubted even once, I'll be certain.

You might as well exchange me for a goat when I start letting

Suspicions take over my soul.

You're not making me jealous by saying that my wife is

Beautiful, enjoys good food and company,

Speaks freely, sings, and dances well.

If she's virtuous, these make her more virtuous.

She chose me. Iago,

I'll see before I question. Only when I question will I get an answer.

And once proven, there's nothing more one or the other:

Let go of love or jealousy right away!

IAGO:

I'm happy about it, for now I have a chance

To show you the love and respect I hold for you

In a more open way. Therefore, since I owe you,

Accept this advice from me:

Watch your wife. Notice how she is with Cassio.

Keep your eyes alert, not suspicious or too trusting.

I wouldn't want your generous nature.

People will take advantage of your kindness. Pay attention to that.

I know how people in this country behave.

In Venice, they show heaven the tricks

They wouldn't dare to show their husbands.

People won't stop doing bad things, they'll just hide them.

OTHELLO:

Do you really think so?

IAGO:

She tricked her father by marrying you;
And when she seemed to quiver and fear your looks,
She loved them most.
OTHELLO:
And so she did.
IAGO:
Well, then there you go.
The fact that she was so young and able to put up such an act...
Her father thought it was witchcraft.
I'm saying too much though.
I humbly ask for your forgiveness
For loving you too much.
OTHELLO:
I will always be grateful to you.
IAGO:
I see this has slightly dampened your spirits.
OTHELLO:
Not at all, not at all.
IAGO:
Believe me, I'm worried it has.
I hope you will consider that what was said
Comes from my love for you. But I see you're troubled.
I beg you not to take my words too seriously.
Don't make it more than it is.
OTHELLO:
I won't.
IAGO:
If you do, my lord,
My words might lead to terrible outcomes
Which I wasn't aiming for. Cassio is a good friend of mine.
My lord, I can see you're upset.
OTHELLO:
No, not quite upset.
I truly believe that Desdemona is honest.

IAGO:

May she always be so! And may you always think so!

OTHELLO:

But also, how nature can make mistakes—

IAGO:

Ah, there's the issue. To put it plainly,

Desdemona ignored many other matches,

Individuals from her own place, of her color, and her status.

But forgive me: I don't clearly talk about her.

I fear what may be going on, but I don't want have thoughts I'll

regret.

OTHELLO:

Goodbye, goodbye!

If you notice more, let me know.

Ask your wife to observe. Leave me be, Iago.

IAGO:

[Leaving.] My lord, I'll be going now.

OTHELLO:

Why did I get married? This honest man surely

Sees and knows more, much more, than he says.

IAGO:

[Coming back.] My lord, I wish I could ask you

To not stress over this anymore. Let time tell.

It is right that Cassio have his role back,

For sure he fills it with great talent,

But if you wish to keep him at a distance for a while,

Try to understand more about him and his intentions.

Take note if Desdemona pushes her friend's company

With any strong or persistent force.

Much can be seen in that. Meanwhile,

Allow me to be focused on my worries

And allow her the freedom to act. I ask only this.

OTHELLO:

Don't worry about me.

IAGO:

I shall take my leave now.

He leaves.

OTHELLO:

That guy is incredibly honest.

He understands people's nature, with a knowledgeable character.

If I do find her unfaithful,

Even though she's as dear to me as my own heart,

I'd let her go, and let her meet her fate.

Maybe, because I am different from her,

I've been betrayed, and in that case my only comfort

Would be to hate her. Oh, the curse of marriage,

That we can call these gentle beings ours! I'd rather be a toad,

Living off the dew of a dark dungeon,

Than share the one I love

For someone else's uses. Yet, it's the curse of the great ones.

The privileged are less free than the lower class,

It's an unavoidable destiny, like death.

This complicated curse is destined for us

From the moment we're born. Here comes Desdemona.

If she's unfaithful, oh, then, heaven's playing tricks!

I won't believe it.

Desdemona and Emilia enter.

DESDEMONA:

How are you, my dear Othello?

Your dinner, and the kind islanders

Invited by you, are waiting for you.

OTHELLO:

It's all my fault.

DESDEMONA:

Why do you sound so weak?

Are you feeling okay?

OTHELLO:

I have a bit of a headache.

DESDEMONA:

Oh, that's just from staying awake too much. It'll go away;
Let me just tie something tight on it and within the hour,
It will feel better.

OTHELLO:

Your handkerchief is too small.

He tries to use it to bandage his forehead,
but it falls to the ground.

Leave it be. Let's go inside.

DESDEMONA:

I am really sorry that you are not feeling well.

They exit.

EMILIA:

Oh! I am glad I found this handkerchief.
This was her first gift from Othello.
My husband tried to make me
Steal this multiple times. But she loves this item so much,
And Othello made her promise to always keep it,
That she keeps it with her always.
I'll get the embroidered design removed,
And give it to Iago. What he will do with it
Only heaven knows, not me.
All I want it to please him.

Enter Iago.

IAGO:

What's up? What are you doing alone?

EMILIA:

Don't scold me. I have something for you.

IAGO:

Something for me? That's nothing new—

EMILIA:

What?

IAGO:

To have a foolish wife.

EMILIA:

Oh, is that all? What will you give me

For Desdemona's handkerchief?

IAGO:

What handkerchief?

EMILIA:

What handkerchief?

The one that Othello first gave Desdemona,

The one you always told me to steal.

IAGO:

Did you steal it from her?

EMILIA:

No, she simply dropped it by accident,

And because I was there, I picked it up.

Look, here it is.

IAGO:

Good girl, give it to me.

EMILIA:

What will you do with it, that you have been so eager

For me to take it?

IAGO:

[Taking it abruptly.] Why, what's that to you?

EMILIA:

If it's not for something important

Give it back to me. The poor lady will go crazy

When she realizes it's missing.

IAGO:

Don't worry about it, I need it.

Now, please leave.

Emilia exits.

I will hide this handkerchief in Cassio's room,

And let him find it. Even the lightest things

Can seem like strong evidence to someone who is jealous.

This might cause some trouble.
Othello is already affected by my manipulation.
Harmful thoughts are like poison,
At first taste they seem harmless,
But they stay in the body
And get ready to explode.

Enter Othello.

Look, here he comes. Not even the strongest sleeping potion
Can give you the deep sleep
You enjoyed before.

OTHELLO:

Ha! ha! Unfaithful to me?

IAGO:

What's wrong, chief? Let's not talk about that anymore.

OTHELLO:

Go away! You've put me in a terrible position.
I believe it's better to be completely deceived
Than to have just a little suspicion.

IAGO:

What's going on, my lord?

OTHELLO:

How should I know her secret, passionate moments?
I didn't see it, didn't think it, it didn't hurt me.
I slept well the next night, feeling free and happy.
I never found Cassio's kisses on her lips.
If the person that is robbed doesn't know what's missing,
Then he is not robbed at all.

IAGO:

It's a shame you feel this way.

OTHELLO:

66 I would rather everyone, soldiers, workers, all,
had a taste of her charm,
if it meant I could stay blissfully unaware. But now, goodbye
to peace of mind, goodbye contentment!

Farewell to the tall soldiers and the important wars
that turn ambition to virtue! Oh, goodbye,
to the horses, the loud trumpets,
the upbeat drums, the screeching flutes,
the regal flag, and the glamour,
The pride, showiness, and exciting chaos of war!
Goodbye to you, loud cannons,
That echo with sounds as fierce as thunderbolts,
farewell! My position, my purpose has left me!

IAGO:

Can this be, Othello?

OTHELLO:

Scoundrel, be sure to prove that my love has been unfaithful.
Make sure of it. Show me evidence,
Or, I swear, it would have been better for you
To have been born a stray dog than face my anger.

IAGO:

Has it come to this?

OTHELLO:

Let me see it, or at least so prove it,
Or face severe consequences!

IAGO:

My good lord,—

OTHELLO:

If you lie about her and cause me pain,
Don't ever pray again. Forget all feelings of guilt!
Do acts so terrible they make the heavens cry,
and shock the world.

IAGO:

Help me, heaven!
Are you a human? Do you have feelings?
God be with you. Take my job.
What a tragic world, where honesty is a weakness!
People of the world, take note, take note!

67

To be honest and straightforward is not safe.
I thank you for this lesson, and from now on
I'll not trust any friend, since trust brings such hurt.
OTHELLO:
Wait, you should be truthful.
IAGO:
I should be smart because truthfulness is foolish,
And loses what it strives for.
OTHELLO:
I thought my wife was truthful, and now I'm not so sure.
I thought you were fair, and now I have doubts.
I need proof: I wish I knew the truth!
IAGO:
I can see, sir, you are overwhelmed with misery.
I regret making you feel this way.
You want the truth?
OTHELLO:
Yes, I must have it.
IAGO:
Yes, but how? How do you want it, my lord?
Would you want to see her with another?
OTHELLO:
This thought brings death and horror!
IAGO:
It would be complicated, I think,
To make this happen. Let's call them cursed,
If they ever show more affection to others
Than to their own love! Then what? What next?
What more can I say? Where is the peace of mind?
Still I say,
If hints and strong signs,
That clearly point to the truth,
Will give you peace, you can have it.
OTHELLO:

Give me solid evidence she's unfaithful.

IAGO:

I don't particularly like getting in the middle of things,

But since I've gotten involved in this situation,

I will not back down. I was with Cassio recently,

And when I was distressed by a raging toothache,

I found I couldn't sleep.

There are some people who speak in their sleep.

Cassio is one of these people:

In his sleep, I heard him say, "Sweet Desdemona,

We need to be careful, we must conceal our affair!"

And then, he would grab and squeeze my hand,

Calling out "O sweet creature!" and would fiercely try to kiss me,

Then he would rest his leg over my thigh, and sigh and kiss, and then

Exclaim "Cursed fate for marrying you to the Moor!"

OTHELLO:

How dreadful! Dreadful!

IAGO:

Well, he was only dreaming.

OTHELLO:

But this points to a sad reality.

It's a strong suspicion, even if it's just a dream.

IAGO:

And this can solidify the other pieces of evidence

That seem rather thin right now.

OTHELLO:

I'll rip her apart.

IAGO:

Hold on, you need to think clearly. We've not seen anything concrete,

She could still be faithful. Tell me something,

Have you ever seen a handkerchief

Embroidered with strawberries in your wife's possession?

OTHELLO:

I gave her one like that, it was my first gift to her.

IAGO:

I didn't know that. However, I saw such a handkerchief

Being used by Cassio today to wipe his face.

OTHELLO:

If that's true,—

IAGO:

Whether it's true or not, if Cassio had any of your wife's belongings,

It adds to the case against her coupled with the other pieces of evidence.

OTHELLO:

Oh, if only that traitor had forty thousand lives!

One is not enough, too weak for my vengeance.

Now I see the truth. Look, Iago,

I take all my deep love and cast it away into the sky.

It's gone. Love, surrender your crown and your heart's throne to hate!

Let my heart fill with this poisonous plot.

IAGO:

Still, remain calm.

OTHELLO:

Oh, there will be blood, Iago, blood!

IAGO:

Be patient, I advise. You might change your mind.

OTHELLO:

Never, Iago.

My thoughts are consumed by revenge.

Now, under this stone-like sky *[Kneels.]*

I commit to my words.

IAGO:

Don't stand yet. *[Kneels.]*

Let the heavens witness this.

Iago surrenders his thoughts, actions,
And heart to wronged Othello's cause!
Let him command,
And I will obey with no guilt,
No matter how violent the deed.

They rise.

OTHELLO:

I return your loyalty, not with useless thanks,
But with generous acceptance,
And will test you immediately.
Within three days,
I want to hear you say that Cassio is not alive.
IAGO:
Your wish is fulfilled.
My friend is dead.
It was done at your request. But let her live.
OTHELLO:
Darn her, that wicked girl! Oh, Darn her, darn her!
Come, come with me, I need to find
A quick way to end the life of that beautiful devil. Now you are
my right hand man.
IAGO:
I'm yours for always.

Exit.

SCENE IV. CYPRUS. BEFORE THE CASTLE

71 *[ENTER DESDEMONA, EMILIA, AND CLOWN.]*

DESDEMONA:

Do you know, Clown, where Lieutenant Cassio stays?

CLOWN:

I wouldn't dare to say he stays anywhere.

DESDEMONA:

Why, man?

CLOWN:

He's a soldier and to say a soldier stays somewhere is risky.

DESDEMONA:

Alright. Where does he live then?

CLOWN:

To tell you where he lives would be revealing where I live too.

DESDEMONA:

Can we understand anything from this?

CLOWN:

I don't know where he lives. If I had to make a guess and say he stays here or there, it would be to lie.

DESDEMONA:

Can you find him and learn from the information?

CLOWN:

I will ask around for him.

DESDEMONA:

Look for him, ask him to come here. Tell him I have convinced my husband for his sake, and hope all will be well.

CLOWN:

Doing this is within what a man can think of, so I will try to do it.

Exit.

DESDEMONA:

Where could I have lost that handkerchief, Emilia?

EMILIA:

I don't know, ma'am.

DESDEMONA:

Believe me, I would rather have lost my money.
If my husband is trustworthy and not the suspicious type
This will be enough to make him worry.

EMILIA:

Doesn't he get jealous?

DESDEMONA:

Who, him? I believe the sun where he was born
Took away all such worries from him.

EMILIA:

Look, here he comes.

Enter Othello.

DESDEMONA:

I'll not leave until I've asked Cassio to come here.
How are you, my lord?

OTHELLO:

I'm good, lady. *[Aside.]*
Oh, it's tough to pretend! How are you, Desdemona?

DESDEMONA:

I'm good, my lord.

OTHELLO:

Give me your hand. Your hand is warm, my lady.

DESDEMONA:

It's still young and hasn't known sadness.

OTHELLO:

It suggests kindness and a hearty spirit.

It's very warm. Your hand needs

a break, some quiet time, and good deeds.

It's a good hand, an honest one.

DESDEMONA:

You're right, as it was this hand that gave away my heart.

OTHELLO:

A generous hand indeed.

Old folks used to give their hearts,

But now it seems we just give hands, not hearts.

DESDEMONA:

I can't discuss this further.

Now, your promise.

OTHELLO:

What promise, dear?

DESDEMONA:

I've asked Cassio to come speak with you.

OTHELLO:

I've been feeling a bit sick.

Can I have your handkerchief?

DESDEMONA:

Here you go, my lord.

OTHELLO:

No, the one I gave you.

DESDEMONA:

I don't have it with me.

OTHELLO:

You don't?

DESDEMONA:

No, honestly, my lord.

OTHELLO:

That's not good.

That handkerchief was given by an Egyptian to my mother.

She could almost read people's thoughts.

She said that as long as she kept it,

It would make her lovely

And make my father love her completely.

But if she lost it or gave it away, my father's eye

Would turn from her

And his mind would begin to wander.

All this she told me before she died.

She wanted me to pass this handkerchief to my future wife.

She wished for me to care for it.

Losing it would bring about a huge consequence.

DESDEMONA:

Can this be true?

OTHELLO:

Yes, it is. The handkerchief is magical.

Years ago, a prophetess who had seen

The world under the sun for two hundred years weaved it.

The silkworms that spun the silk were blessed,

And the silk was dyed and preserved.

DESDEMONA:

Really? Is this true?

OTHELLO:

Yes, absolutely. You should take care of it.

DESDEMONA:

I wish I'd never laid eyes on it then!

OTHELLO:

What? Why is that?

DESDEMONA:

Why are you speaking so rudely?

OTHELLO:

Is it lost? Is it gone? Tell me, is it missing?

DESDEMONA:

Bless us!

OTHELLO:

What did you say?

DESDEMONA:

It's not lost, but what if it were?

OTHELLO:

What do you mean?

DESDEMONA:

I'm saying it isn't lost.

OTHELLO:

Bring it to me, let me see it.

DESDEMONA:

I could, sir, but I won't right now.

This is a trick to distract me.

I pray you, welcome Cassio back.

OTHELLO:

Bring me the handkerchief! My mind is restless!

DESDEMONA:

Calm down.

You won't find a better man than him.

OTHELLO:

The handkerchief!

DESDEMONA:

I wish you would discuss Cassio with me.

OTHELLO:

The handkerchief!

DESDEMONA:

74 A man who has spent all his time building

His good luck based on your love

And has shared dangers with you...

OTHELLO:

The handkerchief!

DESDEMONA:

Truly, you are doing wrong.

OTHELLO:

Go away!

He leaves.

EMILIA:

Isn't this man jealous?

DESDEMONA:

I've never seen this before.

There must be some magic in this handkerchief.

I'm so upset it is lost.

EMILIA:

You can't know what a man is like in just a year or two.

They're just hungry and we're their food.

When they're full, they just burp us out.

Enter Cassio and Iago.

Look, there's Cassio and my husband.

IAGO:

There's only one way.

She has to do it and won't it be wonderful!

Go and beg her to do it.

DESDEMONA:

Hello, good Cassio, do you have any news?

CASSIO:

Madam, my earlier request.

I beg you to help me to be in his love again.

I absolutely respect him with all my heart.

I don't want to wait.

Do you think he'll have me back?

DESDEMONA:

Oh, kind Cassio, I'm not in a position to help right now.

My husband isn't himself.

I swear by all that's holy, I've done all I can for you.
He is in the path of his displeasure
Because of my honesty! You need to be patient.
What I can do, I will and I will do
Even more than I dare for myself. Let that calm you.

IAGO:

Is my master upset?

EMILIA:

He just left us and he seemed very upset.

IAGO:

Can he really be upset? I have seen how scary he can be.
This must be something serious then. I will go find him.

DESDEMONA:

Please do so.

Exit Iago.

Something of importance for sure,
Either from Venice, or some secret plot
Proven true here in Cyprus to him,
Has troubled his clear mind.
That's exactly what's happening.
We must remember that men are not gods,
Nor should we expect from them
Such perfection. Shame on me, Emilia.
I criticized his unkindness harshly.
Now I realize I accused him wrongly.

EMILIA:

Let's hope it's about state matters, as you believe,
And not some misunderstanding or jealousy
Concerning you.

DESDEMONA:

Oh, what a day! I never gave him a reason to be like this!

EMILIA:

But jealous minds will not accept that as an answer.
They are not always jealous for the right reason.

The emotional distress you talk about

Is a beast that feeds on itself.

It comes from its own fear.

DESDEMONA:

I hope that this fear can be

Kept away from my dear Othello!

EMILIA:

Truly, I hope so too.

DESDEMONA:

I'll find him now. Cassio, wait for me here.

If his mood is fitting,

I will mention your issue with him and do all that I can to help.

CASSIO:

Thank you, dear Desdemona.

Exit Desdemona and Emilia. Enter Bianca.

BIANCA:

Hello, my friend Cassio!

CASSIO:

You're away from home?

How have you been, my dear Bianca?

I had planned to visit you.

BIANCA:

I was just on my way to your place, Cassio.

Weren't you supposed to visit me a week ago?

I kept waiting for you.

CASSIO:

I'm sorry, Bianca.

I've been greatly distracted recently,

But I'll make it up to you.

He hands her Desdemona's handkerchief.

Here, I need a favor.

BIANCA:

Cassio, where did you get this?

This is some gift from a new friend of yours.

Now I understand why you were away. Has it come to this?

CASSIO:

Stop it, Bianca!

Don't jump to wrong conclusions.

You think this is a souvenir from a mistress.

Not at all, Bianca.

BIANCA:

Then, whose is it?

CASSIO:

I have no idea, I found it in my room.

I do like the embroidery on it.

If someone asks about it,

It looks good enough for me, I'd like a copy of it.

Take it, do it, and leave me alone for now.

BIANCA:

Leave you, why?

CASSIO:

I'm waiting here for the general.

I don't think it's appropriate, or my desire

For him to see me with a woman.

BIANCA:

Why, I wonder?

CASSIO:

Not because I don't love you.

BIANCA:

But because you don't love me.

Please accompany me a little way and tell me if I'll see you again tonight.

CASSIO:

It's a short distance but I can walk with you,

Because I have to stay here. But I'll see you soon.

BIANCA:

That's good enough. I must be patient.

Everyone exits the scene.

ACT IV

SCENE 1. CYPRUS. BEFORE THE CASTLE

 [Enter Othello and Iago.]

IAGO:

Do you believe it's possible?

OTHELLO:

Believe what, Iago?

IAGO:

What if they kissed without anyone around?

OTHELLO:

A secret kiss?

IAGO:

Or what if she was alone with him in a room for more than an hour?

What if they intended for nothing to happen between them?

OTHELLO:

In a room alone, Iago? And not intending anything?

That sounds crazy!

They tempt themselves and they tempt fate!

IAGO:

If they don't do anything else, it's a small mistake.

But if I gave my wife a handkerchief—

OTHELLO:

And?

IAGO:

Then, it belongs to her, sir, and since it's hers,

She can, I think, give it to anyone she pleases.

OTHELLO:

She also must look after her own reputation.

Is she allowed to give that away?

IAGO:

Her good name is priceless and can't be seen.

Often people who seem to have it don't.

But about the handkerchief—

OTHELLO:

I wish I could forget it.

You said that Cassio had my handkerchief.

IAGO:

Yes, and what about it?

OTHELLO:

That's not a good thing.

IAGO:

What if I had said I saw him doing something wrong?

Or heard him saying things...

OTHELLO:

Did he say anything then?

IAGO:

Yes, sir, but let me help you,

He won't stick to what he said.

79 **OTHELLO:**

What did he say?

IAGO:

Honestly, he did say something—

I just don't know exactly what he said.

OTHELLO:

What? What?

IAGO:

He lied.

OTHELLO:

About her?

IAGO:

With her. You know what I mean.

OTHELLO:

He lied with her and about her! We say he lied about her when he said untruths her. Lie with her! That's disgusting. The handkerchief, the handkerchief! I'm nervous. No one would get so worked up without a good reason. It's not the words that are really bothering me. Enough! Noses, lips, ears. Is this really possible? Admit it? The handkerchief? Unbelievable!

Falls unconscious

IAGO:

Keep it up. Your trick is working well!
This is how people get tricked,
And many good, innocent ladies get accused like this.
Hey! Wake up!
Wake up, I said! Othello!

Enter Cassio.

What's wrong now, Cassio?!

CASSIO:

What's happened?

IAGO:

My lord has fainted. This is his second time. He also had one yesterday.

CASSIO:

You should rub his forehead.

IAGO:

No, don't.

Let the faintness run its course.

If not, he starts foaming at the mouth and then

Becomes utterly wild. Look, he's starting to move.

Please step aside for a little bit,

He'll come around soon. Once he's gone,

I need to talk with you about something important.

Exit Cassio.

How are you feeling, general? Did you hit your head?

OTHELLO:

Are you making fun of me?

IAGO:

Make fun of you? I'm certainly not!

If only you could deal with your situation like a grown-up!

OTHELLO:

A man with horns is a creature and a monster.

IAGO:

Well, there's a lot of creatures, then, in a crowded city,

And many a well-mannered monster.

OTHELLO:

Did he admit to it?

IAGO:

Good man, hold yourself together.

Think that every man with a beard who's just average

Has been in your shoes. There's countless people

Who are lying in the wrong beds each night

Yet they dare to say they're the right ones: your situation is not

that bad.

Oh, it's the worst annoyance of all, the devil's craftiest trick,

To kiss a loose woman in a safe place,

And to believe her to be innocent! No, let me know,

And knowing who I am, I know what she will become.

OTHELLO:

Oh, you are smart, that's for sure.

IAGO:

You might want to stand aside for a bit,
Keep your patience.
While you were here, overwhelmed by sadness,
Cassio came by. I sent him away,
And excused your state to him.
He'll come back later thought, so just hide yourself,
And observe his smirks and insults toward you.
They live in every part of his face.
I will make him tell the story again
About his experience and goals with your wife.
I say, just watch his body language. Have patience,
Or I'll say that you are completely swept up in bitterness,
And not acting like a man.

OTHELLO:
Do you hear this, Iago?
I will be incredibly clever in my patience.

IAGO:
That's not a bad idea.
But keep your cool throughout all this. Will you step out?

Othello leaves.

81   Now, I'll ask Cassio about Bianca,
A woman who sells her love.
She really likes Cassio.
Men and women sometimes trick each other.
Cassio can't help but laugh when he hears about her.
Here he comes now.

Enter Cassio.

When Cassio smiles, Othello will get upset.
Othello's misunderstanding of Cassio's smiles
Will make the story make sense to him.

Seeing Cassio.

How are you doing, lieutenant?
CASSIO:
I'm worse off since you gave me that title.

IAGO:

Continue doing well with Desdemona, and you are certain to succeed.

[Speaks quietly.] Now, if you had to rely on Bianca,

There wouldn't be much luck in that at all.

CASSIO:

Oh, unlucky fellow!

OTHELLO:

[To himself.] Look how he starts laughing immediately!

IAGO:

I've never seen a woman love a man as much as she does.

CASSIO:

Poor thing! I think, in all honesty, she loves me.

OTHELLO:

[To himself.] Now he makes light of it.

IAGO:

Did you hear that, Cassio?

OTHELLO:

Now he insists that he repeats it. Well said, interesting.

IAGO:

She's saying around that you are set to marry her.

Have you in fact planned that?

CASSIO:

Ha, ha, ha!

OTHELLO:

Are you gloating, like a victorious Roman?

CASSIO:

Me, marry her? Impossible. Give me some credit,

I won't do something that foolish. Ha, ha, ha!

OTHELLO:

I see, I see. It's all a laughing matter to the one who's winning.

IAGO:

Indeed, the rumor is that you are to marry her.

CASSIO:

Seriously, is that the truth?

IAGO:

I must really be a bad guy then.

OTHELLO:

Have you tricked me? Alright then.

CASSIO:

This is completely her own idea. She's think I'll marry her, but I've made no such promises.

OTHELLO:

Now the story begins...

CASSIO:

She was just here. She shows up everywhere I go. She even hugged me once while I was speaking with some gentlemen.

OTHELLO:

Her actions say it all.

CASSIO:

Yes! She hugs me, hangs on me, cries on my shoulder, pulls me closer. Ha, ha, ha!

OTHELLO:

Now he tells how she dragged him to my room.

I'm not the fool you take me for.

CASSIO:

Well, I really must avoid her now.

IAGO:

Look who's coming now.

Enter Bianca.

CASSIO:

Here comes another problem! And a fancy one at that. What do you want from me?

BIANCA:

I hope you are haunted by the devil! What were you thinking giving me that handkerchief? I was a fool to accept it. You expect me to fix it? It's obvious you found it in your room and have no idea how it got there! This is a gift from another girl, and you want me to fix it? Here, take your gift back. Wherever you got it from, I won't fix it.

CASSIO:

What's the matter, my dear Bianca?

OTHELLO:

Can it be? That looks like my handkerchief!

BIANCA:

If you want to come to dinner tonight, feel free.

If not, come when you're ready.

Exit.

IAGO:

Go after her, go!

CASSIO:

I have to, she'll cause a scene otherwise.

IAGO:

Will you have dinner there?

CASSIO:

Yes, that's the plan.

IAGO:

Well, I might see you there, as I'd like a word.

CASSIO:

Please do join us, will you?

IAGO:

Alright, that's enough said.

Exit Cassio.

OTHELLO:

[Steps forward.] How do I take him down, Iago?

IAGO:

Did you see him laugh at his bad behavior?

OTHELLO:

Oh, Iago!

IAGO:

And did you recognize the handkerchief?

OTHELLO:

Was that mine?

IAGO:

It was yours indeed. She gave him the handkerchief and he gave it to Bianca

OTHELLO:

I would spend nine years taking him down. What a beautiful woman, how fair, how sweet!

IAGO:

Forget about her now.

OTHELLO:

Let her be ruined, and forgotten, and be held responsible tonight. She will not live. I will resist her charm. Oh, she was the sweetest once! Now what?

IAGO:

That's not the way to think.

OTHELLO:

I'm only stating facts. Such intelligence and creativity!

IAGO:

All that makes her worse, indeed.

OTHELLO:

A thousand times worse, and yet she's so gentle!

IAGO:

Too gentle, indeed.

OTHELLO:

No doubt about it. But it's such a shame, Iago! Oh, Iago, what a pity!

IAGO:

If you're so accepting of her wrongdoings, then let her carry on. If it doesn't bother you, it shouldn't bother anyone else.

OTHELLO:

I'll put an end to her. She's cheated on me!

IAGO:

Oh, she's done a terrible thing.

OTHELLO:

With my officer!

IAGO:

That's even worse.

OTHELLO:

Get me some poison, Iago. Tonight I won't reason with her.

IAGO:

Don't do it with poison, strangle her in her bed, the very bed she defiled.

OTHELLO:

That's good, very good. The justice of this pleases me.

IAGO:

As for Cassio, let me handle him. You'll hear more by midnight.

OTHELLO:

Very well. *[A trumpet within.]* What's that trumpet sound?

Enter Lodovico, Desdemona and Attendant.

IAGO:

Something from Venice, surely. It's Lodovico.

He comes from the duke. Look, your wife is with him.

LODOVICO:

Greetings, respected general!

OTHELLO:

Nicely met, sir.

LODOVICO:

The duke and senators of Venice send their regards.

Gives him a packet.

OTHELLO:

I appreciate their message.

Opens the packet and reads.

DESDEMONA:

What's the news, dear cousin Lodovico?

IAGO:

Good to see you, sir.

Welcome to Cyprus.

LODOVICO:

Thank you. How is Lieutenant Cassio doing?

IAGO:

He's alive, sir.

DESDEMONA:

Cousin, there's been a misunderstanding between him and my husband, but you'll fix everything.

OTHELLO:

Are you sure about that?

DESDEMONA:

My lord?

OTHELLO:

[Reads.] "Don't fail to do this, or else—"

LODOVICO:

He's not calling us. He's distracted with reading that paper.

Is there a problem between my lord and Cassio?

DESDEMONA:

A big problem. I wish I could fix it because I really like Cassio.

OTHELLO:

How shocking!

DESDEMONA:

My lord?

OTHELLO:

Are you serious?

DESDEMONA:

Why are you so angry?

LODOVICO:

Maybe the letter upset him.

I guess they are ordering him home and putting Cassio in charge.

DESDEMONA:

Honestly, I'm happy about that.

OTHELLO:

Really?

DESDEMONA:

My lord?

OTHELLO:

I'm pleased to see you upset.

DESDEMONA:

Why, dear Othello?

OTHELLO:

You're terrible!

Strikes her.

DESDEMONA:

I don't deserve this.

LODOVICO:

My lord, no one in Venice would believe this.

It's too much. Apologize to her. She's crying.

OTHELLO:

Oh, well done, well done!

Tears from women are only a trick!

Get out of my sight!

DESDEMONA:

I don't want to upset you any further.

Leaving.

LODOVICO:

Indeed, she's a well-behaved lady.

My lord, I urge you to call her back.

OTHELLO:

Lady!

DESDEMONA:

My lord?

OTHELLO:

What do you want with her, sir?

LODOVICO:

Me, my lord?

OTHELLO:

Yes, you wanted me to ask her to come back.

Sir, she can turn around, keep going, and turn around again.

And she can cry, oh yes!

Go on with your crying if that's what you want.
About this situation, sir! What a show of emotion!
I've been told to return home. Please, make your way.
I'll send for you soon. Sir, I follow the orders,
And will go back to Venice. Off you go!

Desdemona exits.

Tonight, Cassio will take my position. And, sir,
I request that we may dine together.
Welcome, sir, to Cyprus. What madness!

He exits.

LODOVICO:

Such change in Othello, who our whole council
Considered completely reliable. Is this the man
That couldn't be moved by emotion?
Whose goodness no one could touch?

IAGO:

He is greatly changed.

LODOVICO:

Is his mind sound? Is he thinking straight?

IAGO:

He is as he is. I can't reveal my true thoughts
About what he might be. If he is not being himself,
I wish he would come back to his senses!

LODOVICO:

Did he really hit his wife? Am I imagining this?

IAGO:

Truly, that was not good. However, I wish I had known
That hitting her would be the worst thing he did.

LODOVICO:

Is this normal for him?
Or did the news in the letters arouse his anger,
Creating this misbehavior?

IAGO:

Oh, dear, oh, dear!

It wouldn't be right for me to share
What I've seen and know. You will watch him,
And his own actions will make it clear
So I can save my conversation. Just keep an eye on him,
And see how he behaves.
LODOVICO:
I'm sorry to realize I was wrong about him.

Exit.

SCENE 11. CYPRUS. A ROOM IN THE CASTLE

87 *[Othello and Emilia enter.]*

OTHELLO:

You didn't see anything, did you?

EMILIA:

I've never suspected anything.

OTHELLO:

Right, but you've seen Cassio and her together.

EMILIA:

But then, I didn't notice anything wrong.

I heard every word that they spoke to each other.

OTHELLO:

Seriously, they never whispered?

EMILIA:

Never, sir.

OTHELLO:

Or sent you away?

EMILIA:

No, never.

OTHELLO:

Or find any other way to get rid of you, even for a moment?

EMILIA:

Never, my sir.

OTHELLO:

That's odd.

EMILIA:

Sir, I can confidently say that she is honest.

I'd bet my life on it. If you think otherwise,

It's harming you.

If any person has planted this in your head,

May heaven punish them.

OTHELLO:

Tell her to come here. Go.

Emilia leaves.

She says enough.This woman is sneaky,

Yet she'll kneel and pray. I've seen her do it.

Desdemona and Emilia enter.

DESDEMONA:

My sir, what do you want?

OTHELLO:

Come here, dear.

DESDEMONA:

What can I do for you?

OTHELLO:

Let me look in your eyes.

Look at me.

DESDEMONA:

What terrible idea is this?

OTHELLO:

[To Emilia.] You, come help, ma'am.

Let go of unnecessary thoughts and close the door.

Cough or say "excuse me" if anyone comes.

It's your secret. Hurry up, please.

Emilia leaves.

DESDEMONA:

On my knees, what do your words mean?

I sense anger in your voice.

I can't understand the words.

OTHELLO:

What are you, huh?

DESDEMONA:

Your wife, my lord, your faithful and loyal wife.

OTHELLO:

Keep saying it and hurt yourself.

Swear it.

DESDEMONA:

Heaven truly knows it.

OTHELLO:

Heaven indeed knows that you're a liar.

DESDEMONA:

To whom, my lord? With who? How am I dishonest?

OTHELLO:

Oh Desdemona, go away, just go!

DESDEMONA:

Oh, such a sad day, why are you crying?

Am I the reason for your tears, my lord?

If you think my father is the reason

Behind your recent behavior,

Don't blame me. If you've lost him,

Well, I've lost him too.

OTHELLO:

If heaven had wanted to test me with troubles,

I would have found some patience in my heart.

To make me a target for people to make fun of,

To point their fingers at me...

I could handle that too.

But there, where I've kept my love,
Where I either need to live or...
Be thrown away—
Oh! Change your face to that,
You look like a young and rosy-lipped angel,
Yes, you also look as fierce as hell!

DESDEMONA:

I hope my lord believes I am honest.

OTHELLO:

Oh, yes, just like summer flies in the butcher's shop,
That come to life with a single blow of air. Oh, you weed,
You look so pretty and smell so sweet,
That it hurts to even look at you,
I wish you were never born!

DESDEMONA:

Oh dear, what terrible mistake have I made?

OTHELLO:

Was this beautiful woman, this wonderful person,
Created to wear "harlot" as a label? What mistake?
Mistake! Oh, you common woman!
I could make my cheeks so hot with shame,
If I even started to speak of your actions. What mistake!
Even Heaven can't stand the smell, and the moon turns away;
The naughty wind, that kisses everything it touches,
Is silent in the earth,
And refuses to hear it. What mistake!

DESDEMONA:

I swear, you are treating me unfairly.

OTHELLO:

Aren't you a cheating woman though?

DESDEMONA:

No, I am a Christian.
Of course I'm not one.

OTHELLO:

What, not a cheating woman?

DESDEMONA:

No, I hope to be saved.

OTHELLO:

Is it even possible?

DESDEMONA:

Oh, heaven forgive us!

OTHELLO:

I'm sorry then.

I mistook you for that clever woman of the night in Venice.

The one who got married to Othello—you, lady!

Enter Emilia.

We have finished our task. Here's some payment for your trouble.

Please, lock the door behind us and keep our secret

Exit.

EMILIA:

Oh no, what is this gentleman thinking?

How are you, madam? How are you, my good lady?

DESDEMONA:

Well, I'm half asleep.

EMILIA:

Kind madam, what's wrong with my master?

DESDEMONA:

With whom?

EMILIA:

Well, with my master, madam.

DESDEMONA:

Who is your master?

EMILIA:

The one who is your husband, sweet lady.

DESDEMONA:

I have none. Please Emilia, don't talk to me.

I can't cry, and I have no answer

Except those that come with tears. Please, tonight

Put my wedding sheets on my bed, remember,
And call your husband here.
EMILIA:
What a change indeed!
Exit.
DESDEMONA:
It's fair that I'm treated this way, very fair.
How have I acted, to make him feel
Even the slightest bad thing about me?
Enter Iago and Emilia.
IAGO:
What can I do for you, madam? How are you feeling?
DESDEMONA:
I can't really say. Those that teach young babies
Do it with gentle methods and easy tasks.
He could have scolded me just like that, for, honestly,
I am like a child when it comes to scolding.
IAGO:
What's the issue, my lady?
EMILIA:
Oh, Iago, my master has so badly insulted her,
Used such harsh and heavy words against her,
That any kind-hearted person wouldn't be able to bear.
DESDEMONA:
Am I that name, Iago?
IAGO:
What name are you asking about, fair lady?
DESDEMONA:
The things she says my lord thinks I am.
EMILIA:
He called her a bad name.
IAGO:
Why would he do that?
DESDEMONA:

I don't know. I'm sure I'm not any of the things he said.

IAGO:

Don't cry, don't cry. What a sad day!

EMILIA:

Did she leave all suitors,

Her father, her country, and her friends,

Just to be called a bad name? Wouldn't that make anyone cry?

DESDEMONA:

Sadly, it seems to be my fate.

IAGO:

What a terrible act!

How did this happen?

DESDEMONA:

Only heaven knows.

EMILIA:

I bet some villain,

Planted this lie.

IAGO:

Oh, there's no such person.

It's just not possible.

DESDEMONA:

If there is, may heaven forgive him!

EMILIA:

A noose might forgive him, but let hell torment him!

Why would he call her such names?

Who does she hang out with?

What place? What time? What manner? What likelihood?

The Moor's been deceived by some bad person,

Some known bad guy, some lousy character.

IAGO:

Keep your voice down.

EMILIA:

Oh, I'm upset!

Somebody tricked you,

Made you doubt even me.

IAGO:

You're silly. Be quiet.

DESDEMONA:

Oh Iago,

What can I do to win back my dear husband?

My good friend, please go to him.

I don't know how I lost him.

I love him deeply, but his unkindness might ruin my life,

But it will never ruin my love. I cannot say the word "harlot",

It fills me with dislike as I say it.

IAGO:

Please, be calm. This is just his mood.

State affairs are bothering him,

And he is taking it out on you.

DESDEMONA:

If there's no other reason...

IAGO:

Trust me, there's not.

Trumpets can be heard.

Listen, how these instruments call us to dinner.

The messengers from Venice are delaying the meal.

Go inside, and don't cry. Everything will be alright.

Exit Desdemona and Emilia. Enter Roderigo.

What's up, Roderigo?

RODERIGO:

I don't think you are dealing fairly with me.

IAGO:

What makes you say that?

RODERIGO:

Every day you confuse me with some plan, Iago. It seems to me now that you are keeping more from me than you are giving me even the slightest bit of hope. I won't work with you any longer and I won't put up with your tricks.

IAGO:

Will you listen to me, Roderigo?

RODERIGO:

Honestly, I've heard too much, because your words and actions don't match.

IAGO:

You're accusing me unfairly.

RODERIGO:

But I'm only speaking the truth. I have spent all my money. The jewels you took from me to give to Desdemona might have swayed even the most loyal person. You told me she received them, and made me believe she would consider my proposal, but nothing happened.

IAGO:

Well then, okay.

RODERIGO:

Okay? I'm telling you, it's not okay. In fact, it's quite bad, and it feels like I've been tricked.

IAGO:

All right then.

RODERIGO:

I'm telling you, it's not all right. I will make myself known to Desdemona. If she gives me back my jewels, I'll stop trying to win her over. If not, I'll find you.

IAGO:

You've said your piece.

RODERIGO:

Yes, and everything I said, I intend to do.

IAGO:

Well, now I see you've got some spirit in you, and starting right now, I have a higher opinion of you than ever before. Give me your hand, Roderigo. You have a right to be angry, but I've done my best.

RODERIGO:

It hasn't seemed that way.

IAGO:

94 I agree that it hasn't been proven, and your doubts aren't without wisdom and good reason. But, Roderigo, if you truly have what I think you have now more than ever—a plan, bravery, and strength—show it tonight. If you don't get to be with Desdemona the next night, then take my life with betrayal and plot against me.

RODERIGO:

Well, what do you mean? Is this a reasonable plan?

IAGO:

Sir, there is special news from Venice to appoint Cassio as Othello's replacement.

RODERIGO:

Is this true? If so, then Othello and Desdemona must go back to Venice.

IAGO:

Oh, no. He's heading to Mauritania, and he's taking the beautiful Desdemona with him, unless something happens to delay his stay here. And there's no better way than by getting rid of Cassio.

RODERIGO:

What do you mean by "getting rid" of him?

IAGO:

Well, by making him unfit for Othello's position: end his life.

RODERIGO:

And you want me to do this?

IAGO:

95 Sure, if you dare to do something that benefits you. He's having dinner tonight with a low-class woman named Bianca. I'll go find him there. He doesn't know about his luck yet. If you watch him leave, which I'll arrange to happen between twelve and one, you can take him down. I'll be close to back up your plan, and together we can bring him down. Come on, don't just stand there surprised, follow me. I'll make it so clear why we need to get rid of him, you'll feel you have to do it. It's already dinner time, and the night is wasting away. Let's get to it.

RODERIGO:

I need to hear more reasons for this.

IAGO:

You'll be convinced and happy once you've gone through with it.

They leave.

SCENE III. CYPRUS. ANOTHER ROOM IN THE CASTLE

 [Enter Othello, Lodovico, Desdemona, Emilia and some Assistants.]

LODOVICO:

Please, sir, don't trouble yourself any further.

OTHELLO:

Oh, excuse me. I believe a walk will do me good.

LODOVICO:

Madam, I wish you a good night.

I gratefully thank your ladyship.

DESDEMONA:

Your respect is most appreciated.

OTHELLO:

Do you want to walk, sir?

Oh, Desdemona, —

DESDEMONA:

Yes, my lord?

OTHELLO:

Go to bed right away, I'll be back soon.

Ask Emilia to leave. Make sure it is done.

DESDEMONA:

I will, my lord.

Othello, Lodovico and Assistants leave the scene.

EMILIA:

What's the situation now?

He seems kinder than before.

DESDEMONA:

He said he would return immediately,

He ordered me to go to bed,

And told me to let you go.

EMILIA:

Let me go?

DESDEMONA:

It was his request. Therefore, good Emilia,

Help me with my nightclothes, and then say goodbye.

We must not upset him now.

EMILIA:

I wish you had never met him!

DESDEMONA:

I don't feel the same. I love him so much,

That even his stubbornness, his reproaches, his scowls, —

Please, help me remove these pins —

Seem kind and sweet to me.

EMILIA:

I've put those sheets that you asked for on the bed.

DESDEMONA:

It doesn't matter. Seriously, our minds can be so foolish!

If I die before you, please, cover me

With one of those very sheets.

EMILIA:

Stop, you're just talking nonsense.

DESDEMONA:

My mother had a maid named Barbary,

97 She was in love, and the man she loved turned out to be mad.
She was left brokenhearted. She sang a song called "willow",
It was an old tune, but it suited her sad story,
And she died while singing it. That song tonight
Keeps playing in my mind. Please hurry.
EMILIA:
Should I get your nightdress?
DESDEMONA:
No, unfasten my dress here.
This Lodovico seems like a decent man.
EMILIA:
He is indeed very attractive.
DESDEMONA:
He speaks well, too.
EMILIA:
I know a woman in Venice who would've walked barefooted to
Palestine just to kiss him.
DESDEMONA:

Singing.

A saddened soul was sitting by a sycamore tree,
   Singing to a green willow.
   With her hand on her chest, her head on her knee,
   Singing willow, willow, willow.
   The fresh streams passed by her, whispering her troubles,
   Singing willow, willow, willow;
   Her salty tears fell, softening the rocks.
   Enough of these:—

Sings.

Singing willow, willow, willow.
   Please hurry. He'll be here soon.

Sings.

A green willow wreath is all I'll wear.
  Let no one blame him, his rejection I accept,—

No, that's not the next line. Listen! Who's that knocking?
EMILIA:
It's just the wind.
DESDEMONA:

Sings.

I labeled my love as untrue, but what did he respond?
  Singing willow, willow, willow:
  If I pursue other men, you'll be with other women.

Please, go now. Good night. My eyes are itchy.
Does that mean I'm going to cry?
EMILIA:
That doesn't really matter.
DESDEMONA:
I've heard others say it does. Oh, these men, these men!
Do you really think, Emilia—tell me honestly—
That there are women who cheat on their husbands
In such terrible ways?
EMILIA:
There are definitely some who do, no doubt about it.
DESDEMONA:
Would you do such a thing for anything in the world?
EMILIA:
Well, wouldn't you?
DESDEMONA:
No, not for anything in the universe!
EMILIA:
Well, I wouldn't either, at least not in the light of day.

Who knows what I'd do in the darkness, though.
DESDEMONA:
Would you really cheat for anything in the world?
EMILIA:
The world's a big place. It's a high price
For a small mistake.
DESDEMONA:
Honestly, I don't think you would.
EMILIA:
Honestly, I think I might, and then fix it after. But listen, I wouldn't do such a thing for a ring, or for clothes, or even small gifts. But for the whole world—who wouldn't make her husband look foolish to make him a king? I'd risk punishment for that.
DESDEMONA:
God help me, I could never commit such an act, not for anything.
EMILIA:
Why not? Why worry about a small mistake in a big world when you can have the world in exchange for your trouble? You could easily make things right afterwards.
DESDEMONA:
I don't believe there is even one woman who would do that.
EMILIA:
Oh, there are plenty, and many more who would if they had the right motivation.
But in my opinion, it's the husbands' fault
If their wives cheat: they neglect their responsibilities,
And waste their treasures on strangers;
Or else they become unreasonably jealous,
When they limit our freedom, when they hurt us,
When they cut back on what we once had out of spite.
We have feelings too.
Yes, we have goodness,
But we also have a desire for payback.
Husbands need to understand that their wives are like them.

99

We see, we smell, and we can taste

Both the sweet and the sour just like they do.

What are they doing when they replace us with others?

Are they having fun? I think they are.

And does love cause this? I believe it does.

Is it a weakness that makes them act this way? Yes, it is.

We women also have feelings, just like men do.

Therefore, they better treat us well.

Otherwise, they should know the we learn bad actions through theirs.

DESDEMONA:

Good night, good night.

May heaven help me to not

Pick a bad action from all the bad ones,

but improve a bad action with another action!

Exit.

ACT V

SCENE 1. CYPRUS. A STREET

 [Enter Iago and Roderigo.]

IAGO:

Stand behind this big thing. He'll be here soon.

Hold your sword out, and don't forget to actually hit him.

Quickly, now, don't be scared. I'll stay with you.

The thing we're doing could make or break us, so keep that in mind,

And stay really, really sure that you want to do this.

RODERIGO:

Stay close, I might mess up.

IAGO:

I'm right here. Be brave, and stand your ground.

He steps a little bit away.

RODERIGO:

I don't really like what we're about to do.

But he has given me good reasons for it.

It's just one man gone. Look out, my sword is coming for him.

He gets in position.

IAGO:
I've nearly convinced this young guy to do this,
And he's getting angry. Now, whether he kills Cassio,
Or Cassio kills him, or they both kill each other,
I get what I want either way. If Roderigo lives,
He'll want me to give back the lot of gold and jewels
I stole from him and gave to Desdemona as gifts.
That can't happen. If Cassio doesn't die,
Every day he's alive, I look worse. And on top of that, the Moor
May tell him what I did. I'm in big trouble then.
No, Cassio must die. But I hear him coming now.

Enter Cassio.

RODERIGO:
I recognize the way he walks. That's him. You're going down,
villain!

He runs out and tries to hit Cassio.

CASSIO:
That attack could have hurt me,
If my coat weren't better than you thought.
I'll test yours now.

He draws his own sword and scratches Roderigo.

RODERIGO:
Oh, he got me!

101   *IAGO SWIFTLY LEAVES HIS SPOT, stabs Cassio in the leg from behind, then runs away.*

CASSIO:
I'm terribly injured. Help, there's been a murder!

He falls to the ground. Enter Othello.

OTHELLO:
That's Cassio's voice. Iago kept his promise.

RODERIGO:

Oh, what a villain I am!

OTHELLO:

Indeed, it seems.

CASSIO:

Oh, someone, help! We need a light, a doctor!

OTHELLO:

That's him. Bravo, Iago, you're fair and true,

You understand the pain my friend's wrong has caused!

You teach me, sweetheart, your precious love is dead,

And your cursed fate rushes forth. Deceitful woman, I'm coming!

You've charmed my heart no more, your eyes are a blur.

Your stained bed will soon be splattered with your shameful deeds.

He leaves. Lodovico and Gratiano enter.

CASSIO:

Anyone there? Isn't anyone watching? It's a murder!

GRATIANO:

Something bad has happened; the screaming sounds urgent.

CASSIO:

Oh, help me!

LODOVICO:

Listen!

RODERIGO:

Oh, this miserable villain!

LODOVICO:

I hear two or three groaning. It's been a hard night.

This could be a trick. It feels risky

To approach with help until we're sure.

RODERIGO:

No one's coming? Then I will bleed out here.

Iago rushes in with a light.

LODOVICO:

Listen!

GRATIANO:

Look, someone's rushing in his nightshirt, carrying a light and weapons.

IAGO:

Who's there? Who's shouting about a murder?

LODOVICO:

We don't know.

IAGO:

Didn't you hear someone crying out?

CASSIO:

Over here, here! For heaven's sake, help me!

IAGO:

What happened?

GRATIANO:

This is Othello's officer, as far as I know.

LODOVICO:

Indeed, he's a very courageous man.

IAGO:

Why are you here crying in such pain?

CASSIO:

Iago? Oh, I was attacked by villains!
I need some help.

IAGO:

Oh my, lieutenant! Who are these villains who did this?

CASSIO:

I think one of them is nearby, unable to escape.

IAGO:

Oh, such tricky villains!

To Lodovico and Gratiano.

Who are you there? Help!

RODERIGO:

Help!

CASSIO:

That's one of them.

IAGO:

Oh, a cruel crook! A villain!

Stabs Roderigo.

RODERIGO:

Oh no, Iago! You are so cold-hearted!

IAGO:

Attack people in the dark! Where are these villains?

Why is this place so silent? Help! Help!

Who are you? Are you good or bad?

LODOVICO:

That depends.

IAGO:

Is that Mr. Lodovico?

LODOVICO:

Yes, it's me.

IAGO:

I'm so sorry. Here's Cassio, injured by villains.

GRATIANO:

Cassio!

IAGO:

How are you, friend?

CASSIO:

My leg has been cut deeply.

IAGO:

Oh no, heaven forbid!

Bring a light, guys, I'll use my shirt to cover the wound.

Enter Bianca.

BIANCA:

What happened? Who was crying?

IAGO:

Who was that crying?

BIANCA:

Oh, my dear Cassio, my sweet Cassio! Oh Cassio, Cassio, Cassio!

IAGO:

Oh, you notorious woman! Cassio, do you have any idea

who are the ones responsible for your injuries?

CASSIO:

No.

GRATIANO:

I'm so sorry to see you in this state. I've been looking for you.

IAGO:

Give me a belt. So... Oh, we need a chair,

to carry him with ease!

BIANCA:

He's fainting! Oh, Cassio, Cassio, Cassio!

IAGO:

Everyone, I suspect this woman is involved.

To be part of this mischief.

Hold on, good Cassio. Stay, stay.

Let me get a light. Do we recognize his face?

Oh no, my friend and from my own hometown

Roderigo? No... Yes, it's him! Oh, such sadness! It's Roderigo.

GRATIANO:

What, from Venice?

IAGO:

Yes, him exactly. Did you know him?

GRATIANO:

Know him? Certainly.

IAGO:

Signior Gratiano? I ask for your kindness in forgiving me.

All this bloodshed has made me forget my manners,

And so I neglected you.

GRATIANO:

I'm happy to see you're alright.

IAGO:

How are you, Cassio? Oh, a chair, we need a chair!

GRATIANO:

Roderigo!

IAGO:

Yes, yes, it's him.

A chair is brought in.

Oh, good thinking! The chair!

Someone please help him out of here carefully,

I'll go get the doctor. [To Bianca] And you, Madam,

Don't bother yourself. The one laying wounded here, Cassio,

Was a dear friend of mine. Did you two have any issues?

CASSIO:

Not at all. I don't even know him.

IAGO:

[To Bianca.] Why are you so pale?—Lets get him out of here.

Cassio and Roderigo are carried off.

Please stay here, kind gentlemen.—

Why are you looking so scared, Madam?

Can you see the fear in her eyes?

Well, if you look shocked, we'll find out more soon.

Watch her carefully. I ask you, pay attention to her.

Do you see, gentlemen? Guilt always tells,

Even when we don't speak.

Enter Emilia.

EMILIA:

What happened? Iago, what's going on?

IAGO:

Cassio was attacked in the dark

By Roderigo and some others that have escaped.

He's badly wounded, and Roderigo's like departed.

EMILIA:

Oh no, dear gentleman! Oh no, dear Cassio!

IAGO:

This is what happens when people disobey. Emilia,

Find out where Cassio had his dinner tonight.

What, are you scared of doing that?

BIANCA:

He had dinner at my house, but I'm not scared because of that.

IAGO:

Oh, did he? I ask you to come with me.

EMILIA:

For shame! You shouldn't accuse innocent people!

BIANCA:

I am not guilty, but live a life as honest

As you who are pointing fingers at me.

EMILIA:

Are you comparing myself to you? Oh, the nerve!

IAGO:

Dear gentlemen, let's go and take care of poor Cassio.

Come, madam, you must share another side of the story.

Emilia, run to the castle,

And tell my lord and lady what has happened.

Shall we go ahead? *[Aside.]* This is the night

That will either make me or break me completely.

Exit.

SCENE 11. CYPRUS. A BEDCHAMBER IN THE CASTLE

 [Desdemona in bed asleep. A light burning. Enter Othello.]

OTHELLO:
It's the reason, it's the reason, my soul,
I won't tell you what it is, you pure stars!
It's the reason. But I won't harm her,
Or mark her skin, which is whiter than snow,
And smooth like a well-crafted statue.
However, she must go, or else she'll trick more men.
Turn off the light, and then turn off life:
If I extinguish you, you burning thing,
I can bring back your light,
If I change my mind. But once I turn off your light,
You clever design of nature's best work,
I don't know where to find that magical power
That can reignite your light. When I've taken your rose,
I can't make it grow again,
It has to fade. I'll enjoy its scent while I can.

141

Kissing her.

Oh, warm breath, that almost convinces
Justice to drop her sword! One more kiss, one more.
Be this way when you're gone, and I will do it,
And still love you after. One more kiss, and this the last.
So sweet has never been so tragic. I must cry,
But these are harsh tears. This sadness is heavenly,
It strikes where it loves. She wakes.

DESDEMONA:
Who's there? Othello?

OTHELLO:
Yes, Desdemona.

DESDEMONA:
Are you coming to bed, my lord?

OTHELLO:
Have you prayed tonight, Desdemona?

DESDEMONA:
Yes, my lord.

OTHELLO:
If there are any wrongdoings
That you haven't made right with heaven and grace,
Ask for forgiveness now.

DESDEMONA:

DESDEMONA:
Oh, sir, what do you mean by that?

OTHELLO:
Well, go ahead and do it quickly, I'll walk around.
I don't want to kill you when you're not ready,
No, heaven forbid! I don't want to kill your spirit.

DESDEMONA:
You're talking about killing?

OTHELLO:
Yes, I am.

DESDEMONA:

Then may heaven show me mercy!

OTHELLO:

Amen!

DESDEMONA:

If you say so, I hope you won't kill me.

OTHELLO:

Hmm!

DESDEMONA:

And yet I'm scared of you, you become dangerous

When your eyes start rolling: why I'm scared, I'm not sure,

Since I did nothing wrong, but I'm still frightened.

OTHELLO:

Reflect on your mistakes.

DESDEMONA:

The love I feel for you are my only mistakes.

OTHELLO:

Yes, and for that you must die.

DESDEMONA:

I fear you.

It's not natural to die because of love.

Why are you biting your lower lip so much?

You look terribly upset. These are bad signs, but I hope, I hope

They are not about me.

OTHELLO:

Calm down, and be quiet!

DESDEMONA:

I will be. What's wrong?

OTHELLO:

That handkerchief I loved so much and gave to you,

You gave it to Cassio.

DESDEMONA:

No, I swear on my life and soul!

Bring the man here and ask him.

OTHELLO:

Dear soul, be careful, don't lie,

You're about to die.

DESDEMONA:

Yes, but I'm not ready to die yet.

OTHELLO:

Yes, soon:

Therefore, confess your sins freely.

Denying everything won't help,

Nor get rid of the strong suspicion

That I'm feeling. You must die.

DESDEMONA:

Then, may the Lord have mercy on me!

OTHELLO:

I pray, amen.

DESDEMONA:

And may you show mercy too! I promise

I never did wrong you in my life, never cared for Cassio

More than i was allowed,

I never gave him any special token.

OTHELLO:

By everything good, I saw my handkerchief in his hand.

Oh, you've hurt me deeply,

And you make me call what I need to do

A crime, when I thought it a needed act.

I saw the handkerchief.

DESDEMONA:

Then he must have found it.

I never gave it to him. Call him here.

Let him tell the truth.

OTHELLO:

He has confessed.

DESDEMONA:

What, my lord?

OTHELLO:

That he took advantage of you.

DESDEMONA:

How? Unfairly?

OTHELLO:

Yes.

DESDEMONA:

He won't admit to that.

OTHELLO:

No, he can't talk.

Honest Iago has sorted it out.

DESDEMONA:

Oh, my worst fears are true! What, is he gone?

OTHELLO:

If every hair on his head was a life, my need for justice

Could take them all.

DESDEMONA:

Oh no, he's lied to me, and I'm ruined!

OTHELLO:

Away, cheater! You cry for him in front of me?

DESDEMONA:

Oh, send me away, my lord, but don't hurt me!

OTHELLO:

Enough, cheater!

DESDEMONA:

Hurt me tomorrow, let me be tonight!

OTHELLO:

No, if you fight,—

DESDEMONA:

Just half an hour!

OTHELLO:

Once something's done, there's no turning back.

DESDEMONA:

But let me say one prayer!

OTHELLO:

It's too late.

Smothers her.

EMILIA:

[From outside.] My lord, my lord! Help! My lord, my lord!

OTHELLO:

What's this noise? Isn't she gone? Not completely gone?

I that am harsh am still kind,

I would not have you suffer.

Alright then.

EMILIA:

[From outside.] Excuse me! My lord, my lord!

OTHELLO:

Who is it?

EMILIA:

[From outside.] My good lord, may I speak with you?

OTHELLO:

Yes. It's Emilia, she'll arrive soon. Desdemona is gone.

Is she here to speak of Cassio's fate?

There was a loud noise — Quiet now, like a graveyard.

Should I let her in? Would that be okay?

It seems Desdemona moves again; no. What should I do?

If Emilia enters, she'll want to speak to my wife.

My wife! My wife! What wife? I don't have a wife.

Oh, it's too much to bear! Such a difficult time!

It feels like there should be a massive eclipse

Of the sun and moon, and the earth should gasp in fear at the change.

EMILIA:

[From outside.] Please,

May I talk with you, my good lord?

OTHELLO:

I forgot about you: Oh, do come in, Emilia.

Gently, soon; let me draw the curtains.

Where are you?

Unlocks the door. Enter Emilia.

What's going on?

EMILIA:

Oh, my good lord, there's been a nasty murder!

OTHELLO:

What, now?

EMILIA:

Yes, just now, my lord.

OTHELLO:

It must be the moon's fault,

It's closer to earth than usual

And it drives men crazy.

EMILIA:

My lord, Cassio has killed a young Venetian

Called Roderigo.

OTHELLO:

Roderigo's dead?

And Cassio too?

EMILIA:

No, Cassio isn't dead.

OTHELLO:

Cassio isn't dead! Then murder's all mixed up,

And revenge loses its sweetness.

DESDEMONA:

Oh, I was wrongfully, very wrongfully, murdered!

EMILIA:

Oh no, what's that cry?

OTHELLO:

That? What?

EMILIA:

Oh no! That sounded like my lady's voice.

Help! Oh, Desdemona, speak to me!

DESDEMONA:

I die an innocent death.

EMILIA:
Who has done this?
DESDEMONA:
No one but me. Goodbye.
Tell my kind lord I said goodbye.

She dies.

OTHELLO:
How could she have been killed?
EMILIA:
Who can say?
OTHELLO:
You heard her say it wasn't me.
EMILIA:
She did say that. I have to tell the truth.
OTHELLO:
She must have lied, on her way to punishment.
I was the one who killed her.
EMILIA:
She was the true angel, and you're the evil one!
OTHELLO:
She made a mistake, and she was unfaithful.
EMILIA:
You're the one who's lying. You're the evil one.
OTHELLO:
She broke her promise like a fleeting wave.
EMILIA:
You are too quick to accuse her.
She was completely true!
OTHELLO:
Cassio was with her. Ask your own husband.
I would be the worst person on Earth,
if I hadn't had good reason for what I just did.
Your husband knew it all.
EMILIA:

My husband?

OTHELLO:

Yes, your husband.

EMILIA:

Did she break her wedding vows?

OTHELLO:

Yes, with Cassio. If she had stayed faithful,

even if I was offered a perfect jewel the size of the world,

I wouldn't have exchanged her for it.

EMILIA:

My husband?

OTHELLO:

Yes, it was he who first told me.

He is honest and hates wrongdoings.

EMILIA:

My husband?

OTHELLO:

110   Why do you keep asking, woman? I'm telling you, it was your husband.

EMILIA:

Oh, my dear lady, someone made a joke of love!

Did my husband say she was unfaithful?

OTHELLO:

Yes, woman!

I'm telling you, it was your husband. Do you get it?

My friend, your husband, the honest, honest Iago.

EMILIA:

If he said that, may his soul

Rot little by little each day! He lies straight to the heart.

OTHELLO:

Ha!

EMILIA:

Do your worst!

Your action is as undeserving of heaven

As you were of her.

OTHELLO:

Quiet, that's best for you.

EMILIA:

You don't have half the power to hurt me

As I have the strength to handle the pain. Oh fool!

You've done something and I'll expose you despite your sword!

Help! help, somebody help!

This man has killed my mistress! It's a murder, a murder!

Enter Montano, Gratiano and Iago.

MONTANO:

What's going on? What's the matter, Sir?

EMILIA:

Oh, are you here, Iago? You've done well,

Now others will blame their murders on you.

GRATIANO:

What's the issue?

EMILIA:

Deny this villain, if you're a man.

He says you told him that his wife was unfaithful.

I know you didn't, you're not so evil.

Speak up, my heart is overwhelmed.

IAGO:

I told him what I thought, and nothing more

Than what he found to be true himself.

EMILIA:

But did you ever tell him she was unfaithful?

IAGO:

I did.

EMILIA:

You told a lie, a hateful, cursed lie!

She was dishonest with Cassio? Did you imply with Cassio?

IAGO:

With Cassio, indeed, mistress. Now, hold your peace.

EMILIA:
I will not remain quiet! I have to speak.
Our dear lady has been murdered in her bed.
ALL:
Oh, may the heavens prevent this!
EMILIA:
And the blame for her murder has been placed because of your tales.
OTHELLO:
Don't be surprised, everyone, it is indeed true.
GRATIANO:
A truly odd truth that is.
MONTANO:
A monstrous act indeed!
EMILIA:
Wickedness, wickedness, wickedness!
I believe I sensed this wickedness!
I had the suspicion then. I'll end my own life out of sorrow.
Oh, wickedness, wickedness!
IAGO:
What, have you lost your senses? I order you, return home.
EMILIA:
Noble gentlemen, allow me the chance to speak.
It's only right that I obey him, but not this time.
Perhaps, Iago, I may never return home.
OTHELLO:
Oh! Oh! Oh!

Leaning over his wife.

EMILIA:
Control yourself, don't cry;
For you've killed the most tender-hearted innocent
Who ever lived.
OTHELLO:
[Rising.] Oh, she was unfaithful!

Hardly did I recognize you, uncle. Look at your niece,
She who no longer breathes because of my hands.
I understand how horrific and dreadful my actions are.
GRATIANO:
Poor, poor Desdemona! I find relief in knowing her father is at peace.
Your union brought him great sorrow,
It was the final straw that brought an end to his life. Had he lived,
The sight of his daughter would bring him to despair,
Make him abandon his good side,
And be consumed with regret.
OTHELLO:
Such a pitiful sight. But yet, Iago is aware
That she had been unfaithful with Cassio so many times.
Cassio confessed it.
He said she gave in to romance. I saw it in his hand.
It was a handkerchief, an old keepsake
My father gave my mother.
EMILIA:
Oh no! Oh, divine beings!
IAGO:
Be quiet now.
EMILIA:
The truth will out, it will come out. I be silent?
No, I will talk as freely as the wind.
Let heaven, humans and demons, let them all,
All, all blame and shame me, yet I'll speak the truth.
IAGO:
Be smart and just go home.
EMILIA:
I won't.

Iago tries to stab his wife.

GRATIANO:
What?!

Are you attempting to use a sword on a woman?

EMILIA:

You foolish Moor, that handkerchief you mention,

I found it by luck and gave it to my husband.

He kept asking me and telling me

He more than needed this small thing.

He asked me to steal it.

IAGO:

You horrible woman!

EMILIA:

Did she give it to Cassio? No, I'm afraid not, I found it,

And I gave it to my husband.

IAGO:

Nonsense, you're lying!

EMILIA:

By the heavens, I'm not, I'm not, gentlemen.

Oh, you foolish murderer! What would such a fool

Do with such a good wife?

OTHELLO:

Aren't there stones in heaven to create thunder? Evil villain!

Iago stabs Emilia and then escapes.

GRATIANO:

The woman has collapsed. It seems he's killed his wife.

EMILIA:

Yes, yes. Oh, let me rest next to my lady.

GRATIANO:

He's gone, but his wife is dead.

MONTANO:

He's a notorious criminal. Take this weapon,

Which I've taken back from the Moor.

Come, guard the door outside, don't let him escape.

But we should focus on capturing him.

I'll chase after that evil man.

He's worth nothing but trouble.

Montano and Gratiano leave.

OTHELLO:

I may not be brave,

But anyone, even the weakest,

Can make me draw my sword.

But why should respect live longer than honesty?

I'm done with it all.

EMILIA:

What did your song mean, my lady?

Listen, can you hear me? I'll sing my final song,

Like a swan, and meet my end in music.

[Sings] "Willow, willow, willow."

You man from the Moor, she was true.

She loved you, even though you were harsh,

If I'm lying may I not find peace. As I say this, I know it's the end.

With these final words, I go, I go.

She dies.

OTHELLO:

I have another sword in this room,

It's a mighty sword from Spain, as cold as a glacial stream.

Ah, here it is. Uncle, I need to come out.

GRATIANO:

[From outside.] If you try it, it will cost you dearly;

You're unarmed, and will inevitably suffer.

OTHELLO:

Then come and talk to me,

Or, without any weapons, I will challenge you.

Gratiano enters.

GRATIANO:

What is the problem?

OTHELLO:

Look, I have a sword.

None better has ever been carried

In a soldier's belt: I remember the times

That with this thin arm and this fine blade
I've fought through more challenges
Than twenty times your size. But, oh, empty bragging!
Who can control their destiny? Things have changed.
Don't be freightened, even though I'm armed.
This is the end of my journey, here is my final stop,
The farthest point of my journey's sail.
Are you retreating out of fear? That's a wasted worry.
Just a push against Othello's chest,
And he steps back. But where can Othello go?
Now, how do you look? Oh, unlucky girl,
As pale as your dress, when we meet in judgment,
This look of yours will throw my soul from heaven,
And demons will grab at it. You're cold, my girl!
Just like your innocence.
Oh, cursed, cursed servant! Whip me, you devils,
Away from this divine sight!
Toss me around in winds, roast me in fire,
Drown me in deep pools of burning flame!
Oh Desdemona! Dead, Desdemona!

Enter Lodovico, Montano, Cassio in a chair, and Officers with Iago
captive.

LODOVICO:
Where is the hasty and unfortunate man?
OTHELLO:
That was Othello. Here I am.
LODOVICO:
Where is the snake? Bring the wrongdoer here.
OTHELLO:
I look down towards his feet; but that's just a story.
If you're a devil, I can't kill you.

Wounds Iago.

LODOVICO:
Take his sword from him.

IAGO:

I'm wounded, sir, but not killed.

OTHELLO:

I'm not sorry either. I want you to live.

In my mind, it's a relief to die.

LODOVICO:

Othello, you were once so good.

You've fallen because of a cursed servant,

What should be said to you?

OTHELLO:

Anything, really;

An honorable killer, if you wish.

I didn't do anything in hatred, but all in honor.

LODOVICO:

This bad guy has admitted part of his evil deeds.

Were you involved in Cassio's death?

OTHELLO:

Yes.

CASSIO:

Dear general, I never wronged you.

OTHELLO:

I believe you, and I apologize.

Can you, please, question this half-devil?

Why has he entangled my soul and body like this?

IAGO:

Don't ask me anything. You know what you know.

From now on, I won't say a single word.

LODOVICO:

What, not even to pray?

GRATIANO:

Your torment will open your mouth.

OTHELLO:

Well, you have the right idea.

LODOVICO:

Sir, you will understand what has happened,
Which I don't think you know about yet. Here's a letter
We found in the pocket of the dead Roderigo,
And here's another one. One of them speaks
Of Cassio's death, supposedly to be carried out
By Roderigo.
OTHELLO:
Oh, what an evil man!
CASSIO:
Such a barbaric and disgraceful act!
LODOVICO:
Here's another revealing paper,
Found in his pocket as well. It appears that
Roderigo meant to send this to the terrible man,
But it's likely that Iago came in the meantime
And stopped him.
OTHELLO:
Oh, this harmful rogue!
How did you end up with that handkerchief, Cassio,
That once belonged to my wife?
CASSIO:
I found it in my room.
And he just confessed moments before,
That he purposely dropped it there
And it served his wicked plan
OTHELLO:
Oh, what a fool I've been!
CASSIO:
Also in Roderigo's letter,
He says he hates Iago for convincing him
To confront me during guard duty, which led to
My dismissal. And just now he spoke,
Even though he seemed dead, that Iago hurt him,
Iago set him up.

LODOVICO:

You must leave this room and come with us.

Your power has been taken.

Cassio is now in charge of Cyprus. As for this man,

If there are any cunning acts of cruelty

That can really torment him and for a long time,

Then let him have it.

You will stay as a close prisoner until we get back to Venice.

Now let's go.

OTHELLO:

Hold on. Before you go, let me say a few words.

I ask you, in your letters,

When you tell of these unfortunate events,

Describe me as I truly am.

Don't lessen anything, nor add falsehood.

Tell of one who loved not wisely,

But too much. Of one who was not easily jealous,

But when pushed, became extremely upset.

Of one who, like a foolish man,

Wasted something very precious,

More valuable than all he had.

Of one whose eyes,

Though not used to showing emotion,

Shed tears as fast the Arabian trees drop their healing sap.

Remember to tell this.

And also say that once in Aleppo,

Where a wicked and turbaned man

Insulted a Venetian and the state,

I grabbed him by the throat, and hit him, like this.

Stabs himself.

LODOVICO:

What a horrific ending!

GRATIANO:

Everything that's been said has been ruined.

OTHELLO:

I kissed you before I killed you.

There's no other way but this,

Taking my own life, to end on a kiss.

Falls upon Desdemona.

CASSIO:

I was afraid of this,

But I thought he had no weapon,

For he was strong of heart.

LODOVICO:

[To Iago.] Oh, you cruel creature,

Look at the tragic outcome of this bed.

This is all your doing.

The sight is too horrible for the eyes.

Let this be kept secret. Gratiano, stay in the house,

And take over the wealth of the Moor,

For you are his successor. To you, honorable governor,

Falls the task of punishing this wicked villain.

The time, the location, the harsh punishment,

Oh, make sure it happens!

I will go straight away, and report to the authorities

This tragic event with a heavy heart.

Everyone exits.